THE TRAIL TO THE LAST SHOWDOWN

CLAY EDWARDS—For two years he'd struggled to live down his own legend as a gunfighter. But now, with life and liberty hanging in the balance, he must sojourn through the high country's killing cold, and make death a way of life once more.

C. K. MOXLEY—The cutthroat leader of a notorious bank gang whose lie gave Clay a one-way ticket to the state penitentiary. Safe in his mountain stronghold, the last thing he'd expect is a visit from an angry gunslinger. And the last thing he'd do is let himself be taken alive.

BARBARA LABONDE—The beautiful wife of a battering husband, she vowed she'd never trust a man again. Now she owes Clay her life and means to pay it back in kind. But will she ever let herself echo the love he feels for her?

GENE FLETCHER—The lecherous saloon owner with a craving for the young runaway Clay has promised to protect. When his advances are thwarted one too many times, he'll decide to settle the score— for good.

GARTH CANDLER—The man-mountain of malevolent flesh Clay half-blinded in a prison brawl. He's on the run, too, and waiting up the trail to spill Clay's blood on the Colorado snow.

The Stagecoach Series
Ask your bookseller for the books you have missed

STAGECOACH STATION 50:
BUCKSKIN PASS

Hank Mitchum

™ **BCI**   Created by the producers of
The Holts: An American Dynasty,
The Badge, and **White Indian.**

Book Creations Inc., Canaan, NY • Lyle Kenyon Engel, Founder

BANTAM BOOKS
NEW YORK • TORONTO • LONDON • SYDNEY • AUCKLAND

BUCKSKIN PASS

A Bantam Book / published by arrangement with
Book Creations, Inc.

Bantam edition / November 1990

Produced by Book Creations, Inc.
Lyle Kenyon Engel, Founder

ISBN 0-553-28799-0

Published simultaneously in the United States and Canada

Bantam Books are published by Bantam Books, a division of Bantam
Doubleday Dell Publishing Group, Inc. Its trademark, consisting of
the words "Bantam Books" and the portrayal of a rooster, is
Registered in U.S. Patent and Trademark Office and in other
countries. Marca Registrada. Bantam Books, 666 Fifth Avenue,
New York, New York 10103.

PRINTED IN THE UNITED STATES OF AMERICA

OPM   0   9   8   7   6   5   4   3   2   1

STAGECOACH STATION 50:

BUCKSKIN PASS

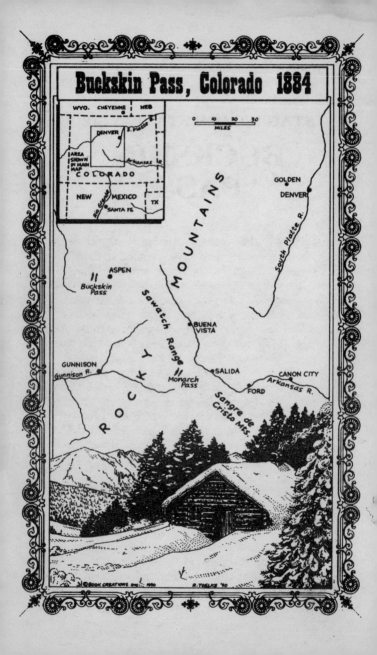

Chapter One

They rode steadily into the sunrise along the banks of the Gunnison River, the metallic ringing of their horses' hooves echoing off the rocks of the immense Black Canyon, which seemed to swallow the turbulent river as it flowed westward. A heavy rain had fallen in the mountains during the night, and a chilly, damp wind blew at the riders' backs out of the dark bowels of the canyon. Ahead of the group of rough-looking men were the distant snowcapped peaks of the majestic Rocky Mountains.

It was early May in 1884, and spring had arrived on time, with the warmth of the sun having begun the thaw some two or three weeks previously. Fed by melting snow, the Gunnison was moving swiftly, and its roar was almost deafening. White bubbly foam outlined the sharp boulders jutting up from its rocky bed and the drifting logs that had jammed and found lodging against its rugged, sinuous banks.

Thin plumes of vapor rose from the travelers and their mounts, for the air was still quite cold that early in the morning at seven thousand feet above sea level. Unshaven and unkempt, outlaw leader C. K. Moxley squinted against the glare of the rising sun, visualizing the town of Gunnison that lay just beyond the rolling hills. At thirty-six he was the oldest of the bunch, and his beefy face was hard and stony from twenty years of bucking the law. Sneering, he thought of the employees of the Rocky Moun-

tain Bank in Gunnison. They were probably rising from
their beds and had no idea that before closing time of this
new day, they would be looking down the muzzles of six
masked desperadoes. There would be no money for them
to lock up in the safe, for the Moxley gang would have
escaped with it all.

Moxley adjusted himself in the saddle, unbuttoned
his plaid wool mackinaw, and thrust his free hand inside
the coat to his shirt pocket. He pulled out a ready-made
cigarette and stuck it in the corner of his mouth, and then,
reaching in again, he produced a wooden match and flared
it with a thumbnail. He lit the cigarette, filling his lungs
with smoke, and then blew out the match and dropped it
into the snow.

A squat figure in the saddle, C. K. Moxley was known
to be tough, brutal, and reasonably fast on the draw.
Though he had not faced any of the top gunfighters of the
day, he had taken out some men with good reputations,
giving him enough prestige to intimidate most of the men
who heard his name.

On Moxley's left rode Kent Landis, who had great
aspirations of becoming a fearsome gunfighter. Recently
turned twenty-one, the black-haired Landis fancied himself faster and deadlier than he really was. Moxley liked
the kid and was worried that he would meet his match
before he saw his next birthday. To Moxley's right was his
own younger brother, Mike, a dark curly-haired man nearing thirty, and following close behind the front threesome
were Auburn Cook, Mel Povey, and Irv Higgins, all in
their late twenties, all of medium height and weight, all
with various shades of lank brown hair—and all hardcases.

Speaking to his men above the roar of the river, the
leader shouted, "We should be in Gunnison somewhere
around noon. I passed through a couple of years ago, so I
know the place. We'll grab us some lunch at the Mountain
Café, then get us a couple snorts at the Bull's-eye Saloon.
The bank closes at three. We'll give the businesses a

chance to make their deposits for the day and hit it about ten minutes before closin' time."

Mike Moxley chuckled and looked at his brother proudly. "That's what so great about ridin' with C.K. He's always thinkin'. I've known of plenty of gangs that rob banks without thinkin' ahead. Most of 'em will just go gallopin' into town, payin' no attention to what time of day it is, and pull their robbery. My brother is as sharp as a honed razor. Wait till the merchants have stuffed their day's profits into the tellers' hands and then hit the bank."

"So what happens after the Gunnison bank, C.K.?" asked Cook.

Over his shoulder, Moxley replied, "We'll hightail it into the mountains and hole up till the posse gets weary of lookin' for us. Then we'll ride over Monarch Pass to Salida. When we've cleaned out Salida's bank, we'll beeline for Colorado Springs. They got three banks just beggin' to be relieved of their money."

Landis looked at Moxley and asked, "How come you're so sure there'll be a posse after us when we leave Gunnison? Them four banks we hit over in Utah right after joinin' up with you didn't produce no posses."

"That's 'cause they were little towns and little banks, kid," answered the thick-bodied leader. "They ain't got the manpower to make up posses, and they figured what little we got wasn't worth chasin' us for, anyhow. Be different this time. I told you, I been to Gunnison before. There's plenty of money in this valley—and only one bank. This'll be the biggest job since you boys been ridin' with me and Mike. Oughtta clear somewhere between ten and fifteen thousand." He nodded slowly. "There'll be a posse on our tails, all right."

"Sounds to me like Colorado Springs'll be even bigger," put in Povey. "I mean, if you ain't kiddin' about us takin' three banks."

"I ain't kiddin'," Moxley said flatly, blowing smoke.

"How we gonna do it, C.K.?" queried Mike. "Surely

there ain't no way we can hit two banks at closin' time, let alone three."

"I ain't got it all figured out yet," admitted his brother, grinning, "but by the time we get there, I will have. We'll probably hit one bank early in the day and ride into the mountains, and then we'll slip away from the posse, ride right back into town, and hit the second bank. What I'm thinkin' is, we might just come back at closin' time the next day and surprise the whole town by hittin' number three sudden-like. I'm not sure yet, but I'm workin' on it."

Mike laughed. "Well, I ain't got the least doubt you'll get it all worked out, big brother. One of these days we'll be so rotten rich, we'll have to open our own bank!"

"That'd be a good one, wouldn't it?" Moxley responded with a laugh. "Open up a bank with money stolen from other banks!"

"Be kinda ironic, wouldn't it," Higgins joked, "if you went ahead and did just that—and then some dirty scoundrels like us barged in and robbed you?"

Moxley laughed, spilling ashes from his cigarette. "Yep, it'd be ironic, all right! I'd raise my own posse and go after 'em, too!"

The robbers continued on, keeping a steady pace eastward. By nine o'clock they had stopped to shed their coats, stuffing them under the ropes that tied their bedrolls to the saddles. It was nearing ten when the gang halted to water their horses at the sparkling river. Dismounting on the bank, the outlaws led their horses to the water while they themselves drank upstream.

Finishing first, Moxley stood back a few feet from the bank and observed the others. His muddy brown eyes settled on Mike, who was just rising, wiping water from his mouth. The Moxley brothers had a strong fondness for each other, and even though the elder of them was his younger sibling's physical opposite in every way, he admired rather than resented his tall, broad-shouldered, good-looking brother. In contrast, he was actually ugly—

and knew it. At only five feet five, C. K. was considerably shorter than any of the other men in the gang, but his thick, muscular, stubby body was far from a handicap, for he was rawhide tough, as strong as a bull, and fast with his fists. Nobody crossed C. K. Moxley and lived to tell it.

While the gang members were walking around, working the kinks from their legs, Moxley approached flinty young Kent Landis and said sternly, "I been meanin' to talk to you about them dumb stunts you pulled back there in Montrose and Paradox."

Bristling like a banty rooster, Landis ran a finger over the fuzz on his upper lip and snapped, "Whaddya mean, dumb stunts?"

"You know what I mean! Pushin' them drifters into gunfights!"

Landis's face colored and anger flickered in his dark eyes. "They're dead, ain't they?"

"Yeah, but you were only a whisker away from bein' too slow for the guy in Paradox . . . and the dude in Montrose was even closer than that. You're lucky you ain't layin' six feet in ol' mother earth, kid. Now, I'm warnin' you because I like you: No more of that."

Landis's face stiffened. "Hey, I seen you goad that skinny guy into a gunfight over in La Sal, Utah! And Mike's told me about other guys you pushed into drawing against you!"

"There's a difference between you and me," countered Moxley. "I'm seasoned and experienced—and I got fifteen years on you. Why, you're greener than spring grass and have almost no experience."

Landis replied tartly, "The only way to gain experience and work the green off is to get into gunfights. You had to do it once, didn't you?"

"Not the way you're goin' about it," the older man growled. "When I was green like you, I let 'em come to me."

"That'd take too long," Landis retorted. "I'm gonna

be a big-time gunslinger . . . and I'm gonna do it before I'm twenty-five!"

"You'll never see twenty-two if you ain't careful."

"Don't you worry about me, C.K.," gusted the young hopeful. "I can take care of myself!"

"It's more than that!" spat Moxley. "Your big mouth and your gunfights draw too much attention to the gang. You need to make up your mind whether you want to be a wealthy bank robber or a dead greenhorn shooter."

Landis shoved his hat to the back of his head and chuckled. "I'm gonna be a wealthy bank robber and a feared and famous gunfighter! One more gunfight and I'll holster my gun with the dead guy at my feet and make you eat the word greenhorn!"

Moxley looked up at the taller youth and rubbed a hand across his chin, the whisker stubble making a harsh rasp under his thick palm. His face and voice angry, he warned, "If you're gonna ride with me, you stop pickin' gunfights. Let 'em come to you. Got it?"

"Well, what if some big-name guy challenges me?" Landis replied stiffly.

Moxley grinned and shook his head. "Big names don't go around challengin' no-names, Kent. But if you keep roamin' the west with that gun slung low on your hip, you'll have your opportunities to face guys like yourself. Let 'em come to you and learn on them."

"Okay," Landis agreed sullenly. "I'll do as you say."

A broad smile spread over Moxley's round face. "Good! Now you're makin' sense." Turning to the others, who stood waiting for his order, he said, "All right, boys, let's head out!"

When the lone rider trotted into Gunnison, Colorado, he noted that the western sky was clouding up. The tall, broad-shouldered man was astride a long-legged chestnut gelding that had a white-blazed face and four identical white stockings. A lariat rope hung from the saddle horn.

The square-jawed cowboy was, at twenty-seven, foreman of the Diamond J Ranch, located at the foot of Monarch Pass, several miles east of Gunnison. His thick, dark curly hair poked out from underneath his broad-brimmed gray Stetson, and there was a look of dogged determination in his dark brown eyes.

People waved to the rider as he trotted toward the center of town, and with a smile creasing his strikingly handsome face, he waved in return. Swinging in at the hitch rail in front of Jefferson's General Store, he slid from the saddle, cast a quick glance at the Bull's-eye Saloon directly across the wide, dusty street, then opened the squeaky door and entered the store. Two middle-aged women were heading outside, carrying packages. Lithe on his feet, the cowboy backed up quickly, held open the door, and smiled down at them. They smiled back and thanked him as they stepped outside. One of them chuckled and said softly to her friend, "Oh, my, my! If I were only in my twenties again!"

The man grinned to himself, then again stepped into the dusky interior of the store. Standing behind the counter was a portly man of fifty-five who stood tabulating some figures while running his fingers through his thinning gray hair. At the sound of the approaching footsteps, Harold Jefferson looked up, smiled, and exclaimed, "Well, if it isn't Clay Edwards! I haven't seen you in nearly a month. What brings you to town, son?"

"Trying to find one of my ranch hands, Mr. Jefferson," replied Clay in a worried voice. "Fella named Lefty Smothers. You know him?"

"Can't say as I do," replied the proprietor. "Might know his face, but I don't recognize the name. Problem?"

"I'm not sure. He went into town alone yesterday evening, and he hasn't returned to the ranch."

"Heavy drinker?"

Clay shrugged. "Moderate, to say the least."

"Have you checked at the Bull's-eye or the Wagon Wheel?"

"Not yet. I figure to do that as soon as I leave here. Thought as long as I'm in town, I'll buy a new bandanna. I ripped up my old one by accident a few days ago, and I'll need one for the next cattle drive."

"Got about every color and size they make right over here," said Jefferson, çoming out from behind the counter and leading Clay to a shelf across the room. Looking up at the tall ranch foreman, he suggested, "You'll need one big enough to tie comfortably around that muscular neck of yours."

Clay picked through the bandannas, finally choosing a large red-and-white-checkered print. "I'll take this one, Mr. Jefferson."

The proprietor carried the chosen item behind the counter and asked, "Want to wear it or should I wrap it?"

"I'll just wear it," Clay replied. He paid the man and began tying it around his neck.

Jefferson leaned on the counter and asked, "How's the job going?"

"Couldn't be better—unless I owned my own spread," he answered, cinching the knot so as to allow the bandanna to hang loosely about his neck. "I hope to do that someday, you know."

Nodding, Jefferson replied, "Yes, you told me." He paused a moment and then said, "But I have my doubts you'll ever be able to realize that dream."

"Why's that?" the cowboy queried with raised eyebrows.

"Do gunfighters ever permanently hang up their guns?"

"I did." He gestured down at his sides. "See? No holster. And it's up to me whether I ever strap one on again, isn't it?"

The shopkeeper scratched his head. "Well, my boy, I've seen several gunfighters hang up their guns—and so far every one of them has put the things back on. And most of them have died with a bullet sucking blood out of their bodies."

"I've made it this far," Clay responded. "I'll make it the rest of the way."

"It isn't that I wouldn't like to see you do it, son," Jefferson asserted, "but a man of your stature is bound to still have eager hopefuls looking for you so they can issue the challenge. After all, how many names are up there with Clay Allison, Ben Thompson, Billy Bonney, Wyatt Earp, John Wesley Hardin, or the Farrington brothers? You know as well as I do that in a list of gunfighters, you'd be at the top. Why, your name's a household word from west of the Mississippi to the Pacific. Men have trembled at your presence and spoken your name with awe since you were eighteen. You think it's going to change now, just 'cause you aren't wearing a weapon?"

"I hung up my gun well over a year ago, Mr. Jefferson. Nobody's challenged me since."

"That's because you've been out there on the range," said the proprietor.

Shaking his head, the ex-gunfighter insisted, "It won't happen, Mr. Jefferson."

"How can you be sure?"

"Easy. As we both pointed out, there's no gun hanging on my hip."

"Yeah, and it seems to me that that's plenty dangerous. Like I say, sometime, somewhere, some well-seasoned shooter or still-wet-behind-the-ears greenhorn is going to pull his gun on you, determined to get to the top of the ladder and his name in the history books."

"Ah, but that's the safety factor. No man can build a reputation as a gunfighter by shooting me down unarmed. As long as I don't strap on a gun, I won't be pushed into using one."

Jefferson scratched his head again, looking at the floor. "Well, I hope you're right, Clay. I've heard of men getting pretty nasty to egg a fella into drawing."

"I've faced nasty mouths—and none of 'em has succeeded," Clay stated. He turned toward the door and said, "See you later."

"Sure enough," replied Jefferson.

The cowboy returned to the street, and his horse whinnied with recognition when he appeared. He was about to cross to the Bull's-eye Saloon when he caught

sight of Gunnison County Sheriff Art Booker and Deputy
Jay Finkle angling across the street toward him. At fifty
Booker was graying and developing a paunch, while Finkle
was thin and just twenty-one. Finkle wore an arrogant
sneer whenever he and Clay met, and this time was no
different. For some reason that the Diamond J foreman
had yet to fathom, the deputy did not like him.

Booker was smiling, a contrast to the sour look on
Finkle's face. Lifting a hand in greeting, he said, "Howdy,
Clay. Haven't seen you in town for a while."

"I've been pretty busy at the ranch, Sheriff. Don't
have much time to spend in town." The cowboy decided
to be friendly despite Finkle's sullen silence, and he flashed
the deputy a smile and declared, "Hello, Deputy Finkle."

The deputy managed a muttered, "Howdy."

"So what brings you to town today?" asked Booker.

"Got a ranch hand missing. Lefty Smothers. Know
him?"

The sheriff shook his head, but Finkle said, "I do.
What do you mean, missing?"

Clay again told his story, adding, "I'm here to see if
I can find him. Have you seen him?"

"Nope," Finkle replied coldly, still sneering.

Clay had the passing thought that he would like to
slap the sneer off the deputy's face, but he quickly dismissed it. "Well," he said with a sigh, "I'd better see if
someone at one of the saloons has. Nice to see you,
Sheriff, Deputy."

"You, too," Booker offered. The deputy did not
respond.

After watching Clay disappear into the Bull's-eye
Saloon, Jay Finkle spit in the powdery dust and said grat-
ingly, "The man doesn't like me, Sheriff."

Booker gave the younger man a sidelong glance.
"Maybe he doesn't like you because he knows that you
don't like him."

Finkle shrugged. "Well, so what? He's a criminal."

Booker's head jerked with surprise. "A criminal?

What're you talking about? The man was a gunfighter, Jay. He's never been behind bars in his life."

"Well, he should've been. He's murdered a lot of men."

Shaking his head and sighing, the sheriff turned and strode toward his office a half block up the street. As Finkle caught up to him, Booker remarked, "Clay Edwards never murdered anyone, Jay. There were always witnesses to his gunfights and the record is clear. He never provoked a gunfight, and he always tried to talk a man into backing down before being forced to kill him."

"Hah! How about the gunfights he might have had when there were no witnesses? As far as you know, he may have shot a dozen or more men in the back—or from ambush."

Booker turned and regarded his deputy coldly. "You have a burr under your saddle or something?"

"Yeah. Gunfighters are my burr. They're just killers who can blow men away and still have the crowd singin' their praises. Edwards has you and a lot of people believin' he's through gunfightin'. Well, he ain't got me fooled. No siree! Once a gunfighter, always a gunfighter. They're like wild beasts that get a taste of human blood. The only way you can keep them from killin' is to kill them!"

"Clay's been around here well over a year, and you haven't seen him in any gunfights, have you?"

"Not yet," Finkle admitted as they reached the office. "But just wait. It'll come. Shooters are animals who have to spill blood. There's nothin' as low as a gunfighter. As far as I'm concerned, every one of them's a criminal . . . and oughtta hang like any other murderer. You mark my word. Clay Edwards will prove my point sooner or later. He's nothin' but a—"

Finkle's words were cut off when an ashen-faced cowboy galloped up, shouting, "Sheriff! Sheriff! You gotta come quick!"

Booker recognized him as a ranch hand from the Circle D Ranch, located about three miles south of town.

"What's wrong?" asked the sheriff as the man reined to a halt.

"We got us a real emergency!" replied the cowboy. "One heck of a fight's brewin' between some of the men, and you're the only one who might be able to stop it before somebody gets killed!"

Booker turned to Finkle and said, "You'd better come along, Jay." The sheriff and his deputy immediately mounted up, and seconds later they galloped out of town, following the cowhand.

At the same time, six hard-bitten men emerged from the Mountain Café and watched the lawmen ride by. "Looks like the law's in a hurry to leave town, boss," observed Mel Povey.

"Probably heard we were comin'!" Mike Moxley quipped, laughing.

"Maybe we oughtta hit the bank right now," suggested Povey.

"Naw!" C. K. Moxley said with a dismissive wave of his hand. "I don't let two-bit lawmen bother me. We're cleanin' out the bank just before closin', as planned—when it's good and full. Come on, let's head for the saloon. I'm thirsty."

As Clay Edwards entered the Bull's-eye Saloon, he was thinking how pleasant it would be to slap Jay Finkle's arrogant face. Pausing just inside the batwings to allow his eyes to adjust to the shadowy interior, he looked around. A couple of men were at the bar and six or eight others were seated at tables, and several of them glanced at him casually.

Approaching the bar, Clay waited for the bartender to draw a mug of beer from a keg and hand it to one of the other patrons. As the bartender turned to the tall rancher, he asked, "What'll it be?"

"Just a bit of information," Clay replied quietly. "I'm foreman at the Diamond J. One of my men went into town last night and never returned. I was wondering if he came in here. His name's Lefty Smothers. Tall, skinny guy, blond hair, somewhere in his late twenties."

"I wouldn't know," replied the bartender. "I didn't work last night." Speaking louder so as to get the attention of every man in the saloon, he queried, "Anybody here know a Lefty Smothers from the Diamond J Ranch?"

There were a few negative mumbles or shakes of the head.

"Who was working last night?" Clay asked the bartender.

"Jake Daniels. He'll be in about two. You can come back then if you want."

Nodding, Clay said, "Thanks for your help. I'll ask at the Wagon Wheel, and if I don't get a lead there, I'll come back and talk to Daniels."

As Clay turned to head for the door, the bartender asked, "Sure you don't want a little snort?"

"No, thanks," the ex-gunfighter replied, looking back over his shoulder, "I don't drink."

"That's solves the mystery, then," said the bartender.

Clay stopped and turned to face him. "The mystery?"

"Yeah. I was havin' a hard time figurin' how you could be foreman over at the Diamond J and me not know you."

"Guess that's why," Clay said lightly. "Thanks again."

He pushed through the batwings and stood there a moment, blinking against the stark brilliance of the sunlight. Hearing the rumble of boots on the boardwalk, he turned to his left and saw six rough-looking men walking his way, the leader being a short, stocky man with a mean look in his eye. Paying them no further attention, Clay stepped into the street and headed for the Wagon Wheel Saloon on the other side and a block up.

C. K. Moxley halted at the swinging doors and watched the tall man walking in the opposite direction. The others paused, glanced toward the diminishing figure, then looked back at Moxley. Mike asked, "Somebody you know, C.K.?"

"Yeah," the gang leader replied, rubbing his nose. "He don't know me, but I know him. He's Clay Edwards."

"Clay Edwards!" gasped Kent Landis. "That guy is Clay Edwards? *The* Clay Edwards?"

"The one and only," Moxley stated, still watching the ex-gunfighter as he moved up the street.

Every eye in the group was fixed on Clay. Irv Higgins said, "C.K., are you sure that's Edwards? That guy ain't wearin' no gun."

"I was noticin' that myself," remarked Moxley. "Don't understand it, but I know Edwards when I see him, 'cause two times I've watched him slap leather. Quicker'n lightnin', he is."

Higgins elbowed the younger Moxley. "Hey, Mike, you and the famous gunfighter have somethin' in common."

"What're you talkin' about?" Mike demanded, looking down at the shorter man.

"He's wearin' a gray Stetson just like yours."

"Yeah, and they got real similar builds," commented Moxley. "He looks a lot like Mike from behind."

"He's gotta have a gun stashed somewhere close by," Landis suddenly declared.

Moxley turned and gave him a stiff look. "If you're thinkin' what I'm thinkin' you're thinkin', forget it, kid. Come on. Let's wet our whistles."

The outlaws entered the saloon, took a table, and ordered drinks. They talked quietly, sipping whiskey, but all the while Landis shifted nervously on his chair and kept looking toward the door. Moxley watched him for several minutes, then muttered, "Kent, I thought we had an agreement that you wouldn't go lookin' for gunfights."

Landis wiped a hand over his face. "Yeah, but Clay Edwards! Do you realize how fast I could hit the top of the ladder if I took him out?"

"You couldn't take him out no more'n you could shoot the moon out of the sky, Kent," snorted Auburn Cook. "You ain't in his class by a million miles."

Landis stood up, fire in his eyes. "Oh, yeah? Well, I'll just show you, Cook!" With that, Landis downed the rest of his whiskey and headed for the door. Moxley called after him, but the youth never broke his stride. Quickly gulping the contents of their shot glasses, the rest of the gang leapt to their feet and followed after him, with Moxley swearing angrily under his breath.

Clay Edwards had left the Wagon Wheel Saloon as soon as he learned that no one had seen Lefty Smothers the night before, and he began going from store to store, hoping to find someone who had seen his missing man. He was just coming out of the gun shop when a sharp voice called from the center of the street, "Edwards!"

The ex-gunfighter wheeled around to see Kent Landis standing spread-legged, his eyes gleaming and his jaw jutting. People started collecting on both sides of the street, their voices buzzing with excitement as Clay walked slowly toward the youth who had called his name.

As Clay neared his challenger, Harold Jefferson's words echoed through his mind: "Sometime, somewhere, some well-seasoned shooter or still-wet-behind-the-ears green-horn is going to pull his gun on you, determined to get to the top of the ladder and his name in the history books." Shaking off Jefferson's dire prediction, and determined to remain a retired gunfighter, Clay faced the young man and asked calmly, "You called me?"

"Yeah," Landis breathed hotly. "And I'm callin' you to face off with me—right now!"

Clay Edwards shrugged. "Well, as you can see, I'm unarmed. Now, it wouldn't help your cause at all to shoot me down when I'm not wearing a gun, would it?"

"You're a gunfighter—which means you got one some-where close by!" barked the young hopeful. "Get it!"

"Was a gunfighter. I'm a rancher now, kid," Clay said softly. "My gun's at the ranch."

"Well, you just came out of the gun shop. Go back in there and borrow one"—he smirked—"and I promise I'll take it back to the man after I kill you."

Clay could feel the onlookers watching intently as he stepped to within arm's reach of Landis and stated, "Forget it, kid. I could outdraw you blindfolded. I've had to

kill too many smart alecks like you in the past." As he
spoke he turned to leave. Then he heard a distinct and
familiar sound—that of a revolver being pulled from a
holster—and he turned back around. He briefly looked
down the muzzle of Landis's revolver, then fixed the
youth with a hard stare.

Landis's face was livid from anger, and he snapped,
"If you don't go get a gun and square off with me, I'll
cripple you!"

Clay Edwards was no man to pull iron on. Moving
with incredible swiftness, he grabbed the youth's gun and
wrist, wrested the gun from Landis's hand, and brought
the butt down on his head. Landis folded like a broken
doll and collapsed, unconscious.

Breaking the revolver open, the ex-gunfighter flung
the cartridges into the dust and then dropped the weapon
beside Landis's inert form. Looking around at the crowd,
he asked, "Anybody here know this punk?"

Across the street, standing in the shade of a porch
overhang, C. K. Moxley muttered to Irv Higgins and
Auburn Cook, "Landis got just what he deserved—but we
need him to pull off the robbery. Go take care of him.
We'll be waitin' in the Bull's-eye." With that, he stalked
off toward the saloon with the other two members of the
gang.

Chapter Two

As Clay Edwards continued on his way, inquiring about his missing ranch hand, thunderheads began gathering and the wind started picking up. Looking up at the ominous clouds, the rancher told himself that his search would have to end soon if he were to make it back to the ranch without getting caught in a rainstorm.

Inside the Bull's-eye Saloon, C. K. Moxley was also thinking about the weather, having heard several customers talk about the impending thunderstorm. On the one hand, a heavy downpour would slow his gang's escape—but on the other, it would also slow any posse in pursuit.

Sipping a glass of whiskey, Moxley glanced at the clock on the wall and noted the time. "One-fifty," he mumbled to the others. "We've got an hour, fellas. Tell you what. We might better stock up on ammunition in case we should get into a shoot-out with the posse. I also need some more smokes. Mike, you and Mel go take care of the matter, will you? Get a couple hundred rounds each for our rifles and pistols, and a couple of tins of cigarettes for me."

Just after Mike Moxley and Mel Povey left, Auburn Cook and Irv Higgins returned from Dr. Clement's office, reporting that Kent Landis had a slight head wound that was getting stitched up. Moxley swore and said, "How long's that gonna take?"

"Just a few minutes," replied Cook. "Don't worry.

Kent ain't gonna let us down. He's just gonna have a headache for a day or two. Edwards really clobbered him."

"Better'n killin' him," mused Moxley.

"Maybe you could make Edwards put on a gun, C.K.," Povey suggested. "Challenge him to a draw for bashing Kent's skull."

Moxley glared at his man. "Landis asked for it," he retorted. "Besides, I ain't fool enough to go up against a man with Edwards's reputation. I like livin' too much."

Listening to the thunder getting ever closer, Clay Edwards decided to head back to the ranch as soon as he had spoken with the bartender who had been on duty at the Bull's-eye Saloon the night before. He took out his pocket watch and saw that it was two o'clock; the bartender should be in. Heading back down the street, he made his way into the saloon and approached the unfamiliar man behind the bar. "You Jake Daniels?"

"Yep," the amiable barkeep confirmed with a grin. "Somethin' I can do for you?"

"Maybe. I'm foreman at the Diamond J, east of here."

"Oh, yeah. Big Bart Jarrell's ranch."

"Yes, sir. Anyway, I'm looking for one of my hands. His name's Lefty Smothers and—well, let's say he likes to drink. I spoke with the other bartender earlier, but he said you were on duty last night, not he."

Nodding, Daniels said, "Oh, sure. I know your man. Tall guy. Thin. Hair like straw."

"Yeah, that's him."

"He was here, all right. Don't remember what time he came, but I had to carry him outside so I could close the place. Drunk as a skunk. I even helped him onto his horse. I'd guess the guy's probably lyin' in a ditch somewhere, sleepin' it off."

Clay sighed. "Well, I suppose that means I can stop worrying that something happened to him. Thanks."

Turning to leave, the tall foreman found his way

blocked by a squat, muscular, ugly man. The man extended his hand and said, "My name's C.K. Moxley. I seen you take out Wade Smith in Cheyenne a few years ago. Also watched you outdraw Kelley Byars in Denver. I've long been an admirer of yours, Edwards"—he then gestured at his table—"as are my friends. How about joinin' us for a drink?"

"Thanks, but I don't drink," Clay replied quickly.

"Well," Moxley continued, staring at Clay, "I'd appreciate it if you'd give me a minute of your time anyway. I'd like to talk to you about somethin'."

Clay agreed reluctantly, and when they reached the table, the gang leader introduced him to Povey and Cook. The ex-gunfighter recognized them as the two who had carried his young challenger to the doctor's office. Running his gaze between them as he sat down, he asked, "That fella who called me out a friend of yours?"

Before either could answer, Moxley cut in. "He sure is, Edwards. We're travelin' together, along with some other guys, and that's what I wanted to talk to you about. I wanted to thank you for not killin' him."

Clay nodded solemnly.

"Kent—his name's Kent Landis—he's just a kid," Moxley went on. "Thinks he's better at gunfightin' than he really is. You sure had every right to put your gun on and drill him."

"I hung my gun up a year ago," Clay responded softly. "I'm not interested in drilling anybody."

Shock showed on the gang leader's face, and it was mirrored on the faces of his two cohorts. "So that's why you weren't wearin' a gun," Cook remarked.

"How come you quit?" asked Moxley.

Clay explained that his desires had turned from gunfighting to ranching, and that he was now foreman at the Diamond J Ranch. He was vaguely aware that a number of patrons in the saloon were watching him with curiosity, knowing who he was, though no one was close enough to hear the conversation at Moxley's table.

Finishing his story, Clay Edwards rose to his feet and stated, "I really have to head back for the ranch before this storm hits."

Moxley extended his hand, and Clay shook it. "That's okay," the outlaw remarked, smiling. "Me and my friends, we gotta go anyway. We got somethin' important to take care of."

It was raining hard at two forty-five as the six outlaws, dressed in yellow slickers and with their hats pulled low, hauled up in front of the bank, dismounted, and then huddled together. Lightning shot across the black sky, followed by the ear-splitting boom of thunder, and the wind-driven rain was coming down in swirling sheets. Except for a couple of wagons slogging through the mud, the street itself was deserted, although a few people waited out the storm in the shelter of porch overhangs.

C. K. Moxley asked Kent Landis, "You're sure you're okay, boy?"

Landis's hat was pressed down over the white bandage tied around his head. He nodded, and water dripped from his hat brim. "I'm okay, boss. Let's get our hands on that money!"

Moxley gazed up and down the street. Noting the townspeople who were sheltered on the boardwalks, he instructed his men, "Don't put your masks on till we're at the bank door. Some of those people are watchin' us."

Trudging through the mud around their horses, the outlaws passed between the hitch rails and then stepped onto the boardwalk in front of the bank. Still huddling close, they bent over, pulled their bandannas up over their faces, and then drew their guns. While lightning and thunder ripped through the rolling black clouds overhead, Moxley pushed the door open.

The Rocky Mountain Bank had four employees: two young male tellers, a middle-aged woman bookkeeper, and the elderly bank president. When Moxley and his crew charged through the door, both tellers were busy with customers, a number of whom waited in line. The plump and matronly bookkeeper was examining a ledger with the silver-haired banker, who sat at his desk behind the waist-high railing that separated the small lobby from the work area.

A collective gasp burst from both employees and customers at the sight of the masked robbers. "All right everybody, get your hands as close to the ceilin' as you can!" the shortest of the bandits bellowed. "We want all the money, and we mean business!"

The bookkeeper threw a hand to her mouth and started to sink to the floor, but the president whispered, "Stand still, Sadie, and get your hands up!"

Kent Landis stood by the door, waving his gun menacingly while hands went into the air and the other gang members went to work. As Auburn Cook and Mel Povey backed the frightened customers against a wall and began relieving them of money and valuables, Irv Higgins and Mike Moxley vaulted the railing and dashed behind the tellers' cages. Barking orders at the tellers, they shoved them aside and began stuffing money from the drawers into cloth bags.

At the same time, C. K. Moxley pushed through the gate in the railing and snapped at the banker, "I want the money in the safe! You and the lady take me to it!"

The bookkeeper's portly body trembled as the president guided her gently ahead of him, keeping himself between her and the gunman's revolver. When the safe had been opened, Moxley made the banker hold his hands over his head while the bookkeeper began filling a large bag with the money inside. Flicking a glance from the woman toward the tellers' cages, Moxley demanded, "How's it goin', boys?"

"We're doin' just fine," came Higgins's reply.

Moxley looked back at the bookkeeper and then a moment later glanced again at the cages, catching one of the tellers cautiously moving behind Higgins's back and reaching toward a cabinet drawer. Swearing, the gang leader aimed and fired, hitting the teller squarely between the shoulder blades. The man bowed his back against the slug and fell to the floor as the bookkeeper and two other women screamed.

Higgins whirled around, still stuffing money in his bag, and looked askance at Moxley.

"He was goin' for a gun in that cabinet!" blared the stubby Moxley.

Higgins looked down at the obviously dead man. His words slightly muffled by the bandanna, he quipped, "Guess he got what he deserved, then."

Bandits and prisoners alike fell silent, and the silence amplified the thunder and the rain beating on the roof. When the terrified bookkeeper had finally emptied the safe and Moxley had the heavy bag in hand, he backed to the railing and warned, "You two stay right there, or you'll get what that teller got!"

Moving beside Kent Landis at the door, Moxley asked the other four, "You guys about ready?"

"Ready!" called Higgins as he and Mike rounded the cages and joined Povey and Cook, who kept their guns trained on the dismayed customers, whose hands were still held high.

Higgins and Mike each handed Povey and Cook one of their money bags, making Landis the only robber who had a free hand. Looking at the youth, Moxley told him, "Okay, lead the way."

Landis turned the knob and pushed open the door, then plunged out into the driving rain with the others on his heels. Suddenly the street erupted with gunfire, and Landis went down with an agonized scream.

"Hold it right there!" a voice shouted. "When we saw you fellas goin' into the bank, we knew you was trouble-makers and got ready for you! Now, throw down your weapons, or you'll all end up like your pal—dead."

C. K. Moxley looked in the direction of the voice and spotted four men partly hidden behind some barrels. His response was raising his revolver and firing a shot, and one of the townsmen grunted and fell. The other outlaws opened fire, dropping another townsman and causing the other two to duck down to safety.

Leaving Landis where he had fallen on the rain-soaked boardwalk, the others raced for their horses and leapt into their saddles, galloping eastward through the downpour while firing over their shoulders. The two remaining townsmen then unleashed a barrage of bullets, emptying their guns at the fleeing robbers.

Angered that the rest of the gang had escaped, one of the defenders growled, "Well, at least we got one of them." The man turned to some other townsmen who had just arrived on the scene, guns drawn, and instructed, "Let's get these fellas to Doc Clement." Indicating Kent Landis's body, he added, "I guess that one over there oughtta be carried to the undertaker's."

Just then Sheriff Art Booker and his deputy returned to town, their black slickers dripping with water. They were stunned to learn of the bank robbery and of the young teller's death. Furious at the boldness and the ruthlessness of the robbers, Booker called for a posse to form, and he soon had a dozen men armed, mounted, and ready to ride with him and Deputy Finkle.

Bending his head against the driving rain, the sheriff yelled, "Let's go get the rest of them!" With that, the possemen, their yellow and black slickers shiny with rain, galloped out of Gunnison toward the cloud-enveloped mountains.

Pulling his yellow slicker closer around him as lightning and thunder played in the dark sky, Clay Edwards trotted his chestnut gelding toward the Diamond J Ranch. He hoped that if Lefty Smothers had indeed been lying in a ditch somewhere, he was sober enough by now to have gotten out of the storm. He came up to a familiar-looking fence and told himself that he was now only a little more than three miles from home . . . warm, dry home.

Suddenly a bolt of lightning came all the way to earth

about forty yards from Clay and struck a tree with a resounding crack. A limb split off in a puff of smoke and fell to the ground. His horse shied and whinnied. Speaking soothingly to the animal, the foreman pushed it onward.

Horse and rider had gone only another hundred yards when Clay saw a cluster of frightened cattle huddling underneath a stand of trees in a fenced field off to his right. Abruptly a lightning bolt seared into one of the trees the cattle were using for shelter, and bawling in terror, they began to run in every direction.

Two more jagged bolts lit up the sky, and a small calf tore blindly across the field and slammed into the barbed-wire fence, entangling itself. Terrified, it bawled and squirmed, ripping its hide on the sharp barbs.

Clay galloped to the spot and slid from the saddle beside the calf, which was pop-eyed with terror, fighting the fence that held it. Talking softly to try to calm the animal, the foreman said, "It's going to be all right, little guy. I'll get you out, but you'll have to be patient."

The seasoned outdoorsman knew the danger of being near a wire fence during a lightning storm. If he were touching the wire when lightning struck the fence, it would electrocute him instantly; but if he waited until the storm was over, the animal would tear itself to pieces. Bracing himself, he went to work to free the calf.

The Moxley gang rode hard and fast out of Gunnison, slowing down just long enough to stuff the money sacks into their saddlebags. The wind whipped at them and the rain pelted their faces, but they held the horses at a full gallop, heading for the Rocky Mountains, some twenty-five miles away.

C. K. Moxley was in the lead, cursing the loss of Kent Landis, when he heard one of the men shout, "C.K.! Hold up!"

The gang leader pulled rein, looking back over his shoulder. Fifty yards behind him, one of his cohorts was on the ground, clearly in pain, with the others gathered around him. Pivoting his horse, Moxley spurred the animal and hurried back. When he realized that the man on the ground was his brother, his heart started beating faster. Sliding to a muddy halt, he leapt from his horse and elbowed the other men out of the way, then dropped to his knees beside Mike.

"What's wrong?" Moxley asked, looking his brother over.

The younger Moxley gritted his teeth and gasped, "I got hit back there in town, C.K.! I was tryin' not to let on, but—"

"Where are you hit?" cut in the gang leader, worry evident on his ugly face.

"On the left side . . . underneath my arm. I . . . I don't think it's too bad. Like I said, I was tryin' not to let on, but my head went to reelin', and I fell out of the saddle."

Moxley carefully raised his brother's arm to examine the wound. The yellow slicker was stained with blood around a rip four inches below the armpit. "Can't tell much this way, kid," the outlaw stated in a concerned voice. "I'll have to open up the slicker and take a look."

Illuminated by flashes of lightning, C. K. Moxley examined his brother. It seemed to be only a flesh wound, and the bullet had passed on through. "Look, Mike," he said, sighing with relief, "it don't look too bad. It only creased your skin. Try and hold your bandanna next to it to stop the bleedin'. We've got to keep goin'. That posse'll be on our tails any time."

"Sure," Mike agreed, gritting his teeth.

Minutes later Mike Moxley was back in the saddle. Gripping the saddle horn with his right hand and the reins with his left, he said in a less than firm voice, "Okay, I'm ready. Let's go."

C. K. Moxley peered westward through the rain, half expecting to see riders thundering toward them, but there was nothing to be seen. Mounting up, he again led his men toward the mountains at full speed.

Mike held on for another fifteen minutes before slumping over in the saddle. His horse immediately began to slow, and he called to his brother; then Moxley and the others halted and came back. The squat outlaw man drew alongside his tall brother and laid a loving hand on his shoulder. "I know it hurts, kid, but we gotta keep goin'," Moxley declared. "If we don't, that posse'll ride us down."

Mike sat up straighter and said, "I can't go on, C.K. You guys take off and get away."

"Hey, little brother," Moxley said tenderly, "ain't no way I'm gonna leave you to the law."

Mike began looking around. "Maybe I can find me some place to hide where the law won't get me," he offered. Then, squinting and peering through the driving rain, he pointed to a draw to the right of the road. "Look, C.K.," he remarked in a pained voice. "I'll hole up there."

Moxley gazed where his brother was pointing. In the draw was a barely visible abandoned shack surrounded by tall weeds.

"I'll stay in the shack and tend to this wound," Mike stated. "Like you say, it ain't too bad. But right now, I just can't ride no more. I'll pass out again if I keep goin', and put all the rest of you in danger."

Moxley shot a quick glance westward. He could almost feel the breath of the posse on his rain-soaked face. Staring into his brother's eyes, he asked pointedly, "You really think you'll be all right?"

"Sure. You guys keep goin'. I'll get the bleedin' stopped, give it a day or two to start healin', and then I'll be right behind you. I'll meet you in Colorado Springs in a week or so."

Looking around at the others, Moxley queried, "What do you guys think? Should we leave him?"

"Mike's got good sense, C.K.," spoke up Mel Povey. "He knows what's best for himself."

"He's tough, C.K.," said Auburn Cook. "If he says he'll be ready to ride in a couple of days, then he will. Right now, we'd best hightail it, or what we decide won't make no difference anyway. It'll be jail and a rope for all of us."

C. K. Moxley leaned from the saddle, embraced his brother, then watched him ride down the muddy side of the gully toward the shack. After taking another look behind him, he spurred his animal, and the rest of the gang followed as he led them at breakneck speed toward the Rockies.

Soon the horses were gasping for breath. Moxley shouted to the others, "Better slow down for a few minutes, boys! Let these animals take a breather! If one of 'em goes out from under us, we're in deep trouble!" He looked back over their trail. "Besides, the way this rain's fallin', maybe our tracks'll soon be washed away."

The rain continued to beat down on them, and the lightning lit up the sky repeatedly as the outlaws walked their horses. Soon they caught sight of a man in a yellow slicker who was just freeing a calf from a barbed-wire fence. The calf then ran toward the rest of the herd, collected in the middle of the field.

When the tall man stood up and turned toward them, Irv Higgins gasped and whispered hoarsely, "C.K.! It's Clay Edwards!"

Keeping his voice low, Moxley ordered, "You guys let me do the talkin'. It sure wouldn't be no good if he was to get suspicious about us."

Clay was swinging into his saddle as the outlaws drew up. "Howdy, Moxley," he said amiably. "Right bad weather to be riding in if you don't have to."

"Got business in Salida," Moxley told him. "Gotta keep movin', rain or shine. That one of your calves you was helpin' out?"

"No. This is the Bar X spread. My ranch, the Diamond J, is three miles straight ahead. Guess we may as well ride along together till we get there."

Moxley looked around at his men and hoped the message in his eyes was clear: As much as they wanted to put the horses to a gallop, they would have to bide their time anyway, since the animals needed to go slowly for a while or they would founder. After the Diamond J Ranch, they would again hightail it. "Sure," he finally said, smiling at the ex-gunfighter. "You're welcome to ride along with us."

Sheriff Art Booker and his posse had stopped for a few minutes to give their horses a breather, but they were once again galloping at full speed as they passed the draw where Mike Moxley was holed up in the old shack. Soon Booker caught sight of a group of riders up ahead, and it was clear that the gang could not hear the hooves of the posse's horses because of the rumbling thunder.

Booker raised a hand, signaling his men to stop. Pulling them quickly into a stand of trees, he told them, "Okay, men, that's gotta be them up ahead since there's five of 'em in yellow slickers—just like the witnesses described. They're making it nice and easy for us, since they're keepin' their horses at a walk, so let's take advantage of it before they start running again."

Quickly dividing the posse into two groups, Booker sent Deputy Jay Finkle with one group to make a wide circle around the bank robbers and come out ahead of them. After giving the deputy time to get his men in place, the sheriff would bring his group from behind. When Booker and his bunch galloped in behind the robbers, Finkle and his men would close in from the front. They would surround the outlaws, and if any of the gang tried to make a break for it, the possemen were to shoot to kill.

The outlaws had ridden a couple of miles with Clay Edwards when C. K. Moxley took another furtive look over his shoulder. He was relieved that there was still no posse in sight. Making idle conversation with Clay, the gang leader said, "I heard you askin' the bartender in the Bull's-eye about a ranch hand you were lookin' for. You find him?"

"Nope, but since I now know he went on a drunk, I'm not too worried. I'm sure he'll show up." He shrugged, adding, "Might already be at the ranch by now. By the way, speaking of the ranch, our property begins right here. The gate's another mile up the road."

"How many acres does the Diamond J cover?" asked Moxley, raising his voice to be heard over the noise of the storm.

"Six thousand," replied Clay.

A long, loud clap of thunder sounded, and its boom was just dying out when suddenly a band of riders brandishing guns came swooping over a low ridge ahead of them. Moxley swore, pulled rein, and looked behind him to see another band coming on fast through the driving rain.

"Posse!" shouted Irv Higgins. "I'm gettin' outta here!"

"We can't make it!" Moxley retorted. "We're outnumbered! Best thing to do is surrender! We'll escape once we're in the Gunnison jail!"

"I ain't goin' to no jail even for five minutes!" yelled Higgins. "I'm makin' my break right now!"

Clay Edwards sat in his saddle, clearly dumbfounded, watching the divided posse close in.

His horse dancing under him, Moxley railed at Higgins, "We need to stick together!"

Swearing at Moxley, Higgins bellowed, "As far as I'm concerned, it's every man for himself!" Even as he spoke, the outlaw rammed his spurs into his horse's flanks and sent the animal galloping westward.

Auburn Cook and Mel Povey then looked at each other and nodded. Goading their mounts, they took off immediately behind Higgins. Moxley's heart was pumping madly, and he screamed after the three men deserting him, "You dirty traitors! You dirty rotten traitors!"

Swerving, Jay Finkle led his possemen after the fleeing riders, guns blazing. When Cook and Povey peeled out of their saddles, riddled with bullets, Higgins dropped his gun and threw up his hands.

Sheriff Booker and the others closed in on Moxley and Clay. His revolver trained on them, the lawman shouted, "Drop your weapons and get your hands up!" The outlaw threw his guns in the mud and then raised his hands. Staring at Clay, Booker's face reflected his rage, and he snarled, "I said drop your gun and get your hands in the air, Edwards!"

The stunned ranch foreman scowled at the lawman. His temper was evident in his voice as he retorted, "I'm not wearing a gun, Sheriff—and I don't know what this is all about!"

Booker's eyes flashed and he snapped, "I'll just bet you don't! I said get those hands up—and if you're not wearin' a gun, it's only 'cause you lost it after you robbed the bank!"

"When I what? Sheriff, what on earth are you talking about?"

Before Booker could reply, Finkle and his men returned, holding their guns on Irv Higgins. Moxley glared at Higgins, and fury was on his face and in his voice. "Higgins, you filthy Judas, I'll kill you if it's the last thing I do!"

Finkle ordered the gang leader to keep his mouth shut and then told Booker that the other outlaws were dead. The older lawman responded dryly, "Well, that's half of 'em we won't have to take to court."

"Sheriff, what's this about a bank robbery?" Clay asked again, bending his head against a gust of wind-whipped rain.

Booker assessed the rancher coldly, then rasped, "Look, Edwards, quit playing games. You're well aware that six masked men in yellow slickers held up the bank just before closing time. One of them was shot and killed in the getaway, leaving five—the two we just shot down and the three of you."

Clay immediately protested his innocence, explaining that he was traveling alone toward the Diamond J when Moxley and his three friends came riding up.

Listening to the ex-gunfighter attempt to convince the lawmen, C. K. Moxley started thinking fast. Here was a perfect opportunity to protect his younger brother: Mike and Clay resembled each other, wore yellow slickers, and had gray Stetsons. Since Mike had worn a bandanna over his face during the holdup and his hat had been pulled low, no one could identify him. Why not make the law think it was the cowboy? That way nobody would go looking for Mike.

Clay was explaining about freeing the calf from the fence and meeting up with Moxley and his men. "You've got to believe me, Sheriff! Even though it looks like I'm riding with these men, I don't know anything about the bank robbery. I swear I don't!"

"Aw, quit lyin', Edwards!" Deputy Finkle shot back. "Consider yourself lucky. At least you're one of the ones still alive."

"I'm telling you, I wasn't in on the robbery!" countered Clay, his voice rising with anger.

"What do you take us for, Edwards?" Booker snapped. "You think we're a bunch of imbeciles? We all know how good you are with a gun. So you decided to use it for more than fast draws, eh? Well, we can all add three and three. It makes six . . . and that makes you a bank robber!"

"More than that!" Finkle added. "One of the tellers is dead, so that makes you a murderer—just like I always figured you were!"

Clay Edwards's cheeks were flushed with rage. His eyes blazing, he shouted, "I'm no murderer! I'm telling you, I had nothing to do with it!"

"Aw, you may as well quit alibiin', Clay," C. K. Moxley suddenly cut in. "They've got us cold. Jawin' about it ain't gonna help. You was in on this thing with us. No sense denyin' it."

Deputy Jay Finkle laughed gleefully. "Guess we got you now, Edwards. Even your pal won't help you."

Clay glared hotly at the outlaw leader. "You lying snake! What did I do to—"

"That's enough!" shouted Booker. "Cuff them, men! And a couple of you pick up those bodies and put them on their horses."

While the handcuffs were being placed on the wrists of the three men, Moxley caught Higgins's eye, silently warning him not to speak up and clear Edwards. As Moxley was already furious with Higgins for attempting to get away, the murderous look the gang leader gave him was apparently enough to keep him quiet and help protect Mike Moxley.

"Sheriff," Clay Edwards said in a pleading voice, "I'm telling you, you're making a mistake. Moxley's lying. I don't know why he wants me implicated in this thing, but I wasn't in on the robbery."

"Six yellow slickers, six masked men," Booker said evenly.

"Half of this posse is wearing yellow slickers!" remonstrated Clay. "Does that implicate any of them?"

"I'm not going to argue with you about it, Edwards," replied Booker stiffly. "We caught you redhanded with the rest of the gang. If you were in my boots, how would you look at it?" He shook his head. "I repeat, we got you redhanded. Anything more you got to say you can tell to the judge."

A jagged streak of lightning flashed as the prisoners and the posse headed back toward Gunnison. Pulling alongside his boss, Deputy Jay Finkle turned to the sheriff and said, "See there? What did I tell you! All gunfighters are criminals!"

Chapter Three

C. K. Moxley and Irv Higgins shared the same cell at the Gunnison jail, while Clay Edwards occupied an adjacent one. During the ten days that passed while they waited for the circuit judge to arrive, Clay continually pleaded with the two outlaws to clear him.

Higgins knew Moxley would batter him to a pulp if he spoke up in the ex-gunfighter's defense, and since he was already relieved that Moxley had not killed him for trying to desert, he kept silent. Unable to budge Higgins, Clay pressed Moxley for the reason he had implicated him and about who the sixth man really was, but the gang leader would not give him answers.

On the morning their trial was to be held, Deputy Jay Finkle brought their breakfasts as usual. When he shoved Clay's tray through the space under the cell door, the rancher demanded, "I want to see the sheriff privately to talk to him."

The deputy stared at him, then said tartly, "He doesn't have time to see you."

His blue eyes sparking with anger, Clay shouted, "I'm a prisoner in this jail, and I have a right to talk to him! You tell him—"

"What's going on in here?" blustered Sheriff Art Booker, rushing through the door from the office.

Forcing himself to control his temper, Clay told the

sheriff, "I need to talk with you, but your deputy said you were too busy."

"Well, he is!" growled Finkle. "Any talkin' you have to do can be to the judge!"

Clay lanced the deputy with a cold stare and then looked back at Booker. The sheriff sighed. "All right. As soon as you eat your breakfast."

"I want justice, not food. I want to talk to you now!" Clay responded quickly.

As Clay was being ushered to the office, C. K. Moxley called after him, "Ain't gonna do no good, Edwards! You're goin' to trial same as us!"

When the jail area was clear, Irv Higgins asked, "When are you plannin' on bustin' us outta here, C.K.?"

"There ain't no us!" snapped Moxley. "I'm gonna make a break when we're on our way to the prison in Canon City, but I sure ain't takin' no Judas with me."

"What makes you so sure we'll be goin' to Canon City?" queried Higgins. "That bank teller was killed durin' the holdup. We're probably gonna hang."

"Nah! Things are changin' in these parts. They don't hang people as much as they used to. We'll probably get life. But C.K. Moxley ain't gonna serve no time. I'm bustin' out to join Mike in Colorado Springs. He's got to be wonderin' where we are, but he won't have to wonder much longer, and then we'll head west." He stared coldly at his former friend, adding, "Too bad you won't be joinin' us." Moxley then turned away and lay down on the hard cot, a small smile on his lips.

In the office a handcuffed Clay Edwards was seated in front of the sheriff's desk while Jay Finkle busied himself elsewhere. Booker sat down, looked directly at his prisoner, and muttered, "If it's more talk about being innocent, Edwards, forget it."

"I can't forget it, Sheriff," Clay retorted, leaning forward in the chair. "I am innocent, and you've got to listen to me."

Booker swore, banged his fist on the desk, and spat, "Come on! You were caught redhanded!"

"Seems to me redhanded should mean you caught me pulling the robbery. But you didn't. If I can convince you that I'm telling the truth, you can help me in that courtroom."

"Look, shooter," the sheriff said disparagingly, "your boss has been in here three times, and he got nowhere."

"Mr. Jarrell tried to pursuade you because he believes me. I've worked for him for a year and a half, and he knows me well by now. When I told him what happened, he had no doubt that Moxley framed me for some reason. You've got to see that Moxley's covering for the real man in his gang—the one who got away."

Booker shook his head slowly, his face filled with disgust. "Edwards," he said, leaning his elbows on the desk, "I might just as well give it to you like you're going to hear it in the trial. In the past ten days several men told me that they saw you sitting in the Bull's-eye drinking with Moxley and his men shortly before the bank was held up. That clinches it for me."

Clay felt his face flush with anger. He had forgotten that he had spent a few minutes talking to Moxley in the saloon, and he realized that that innocent act now added to his incrimination. His voice was bitter as he stated, "I don't drink, and you know it! Moxley called me to his table to thank me for not killing that punk friend of his."

"Landis?"

"Yes."

"I heard about that incident, but the way I see it, you and Landis must have had some kind of problem between you in your gunfighting days—even though you pretended not to know him. People on the street said he called you by name before the tussle took place."

"You know how it is with a gunfighter," Clay said, exasperated. "Lots of people know my name."

Standing, Booker mocked, "Well, the judge is going

to know it real good within a couple of hours. Time to go back to your cell."

Judge William F. Klatt was a portly, bald-headed man of sixty. Clad in his long black robe, he banged his gavel on the desk at exactly nine o'clock that morning and declared the trial in session. Sitting toward the front of the packed town hall that served as the courtroom was Bart Jarrell, the tall and barrel-chested owner of the Diamond J Ranch.

Facing the judge's bench, the three prisoners sat on straight-backed chairs to one side of the room, near the jury box. Their hands were handcuffed, and they were flanked by the sheriff and his deputy.

The first witnesses were the bank employees, who testified that there were six masked robbers in yellow slickers, and that the shortest one gunned down the teller. After Sheriff Art Booker testified that the three outlaws who had been killed by the posse were all taller than C. K. Moxley, it was evident that the gang leader was the man who had killed the teller.

Jake Daniels, the bartender from the Bull's-eye Saloon, testified that he saw Clay Edwards in conversation with Moxley and a few others just prior to the robbery. A number of other townsmen then corroborated the bartender's testimony.

The jury retired to arrive at a verdict. Returning in less than ten minutes, they pronounced Clay Edwards and Irv Higgins guilty of bank robbery, while C. K. Moxley was found guilty of murder and bank robbery.

Hearing the verdict, Clay Edwards leapt to his feet and ran to the judge's desk, shouting, "No! I'm innocent! Moxley and Higgins are covering for somebody who was with them in the robbery! I wasn't even in town when it happened! You've got to believe me!"

The judge banged the gavel on the desk and blared, "You are out of order, Edwards! Sheriff, take this man back to his seat!"

Catching up with Clay and flanking him, Booker and Finkle grabbed him by the arms and dragged him toward his chair. C. K. Moxley suddenly jumped up and exclaimed, "He's lyin', Judge! He's been workin' with us, plannin' the robbery for weeks . . . and he helped us pull it off! Ask anybody who was in the bank! They'll tell you that one of the gang was a tall, broad-shouldered man wearin' a gray Stetson!"

The robbery victims all began speaking at once, declaring that what Moxley was saying was true. Judge Klatt banged the gavel repeatedly, demanding order in the courtroom. When order had been restored, he looked toward Art Booker and said, "Sheriff, will you and your deputy escort the defendants to the bench?"

His heart pounding and his face stiff, Clay Edwards stepped to the bench and stood beside C. K. Moxley and Irv Higgins. Moxley grinned slyly, and Clay glared at the man with burning eyes.

Regarding the prisoners sternly, Judge Klatt announced, "Clay Edwards and Irv Higgins, you have been duly tried and convicted of robbery, and such a crime in this state carries a maximum penalty of twenty years in prison."

Clay Edwards felt as though the blood had drained from his body. Then Klatt went on, "Since you are both young men without prior convictions, and since our penal system has had some success in rehabilitating some criminals, I am going to go lighter on you and hope the sentence I give will serve to make you responsible citizens by the time you are released. Therefore, I hereby sentence you both to ten years at the Colorado State Penitentiary at Canon City. Parole will not be considered until you have served half of this time with a perfect record of good behavior."

Clay swallowed with difficulty, feeling almost numb with disbelief.

Klatt then stared at the gang leader and said tightly, "C. K. Moxley, you have been duly tried and convicted of robbery and murder. The greater crime, murder, carries a maximum of death by hanging. I hereby sentence you to hang by the neck until you are dead. Such sentence is to be carried out under the authority of Gunnison County Sheriff Arthur Booker tomorrow morning at eight o'clock."

Moxley was clearly shocked at the sentence, for he gasped and his face went white. Clay, however, felt a small ray of hope: Once Moxley was dead, Higgins would have nothing more to fear—and perhaps he would then tell the truth. But if he did not, Clay had no other recourse. He stood convicted and sentenced, and it would be useless to further try to convince the authorities of his innocence. He would be transported to Canon City the day after next to begin his ten-year prison term.

The next morning Sheriff Art Booker and his deputy walked into the cell area and stood before the bars. The sheriff looked at Clay Edwards and Irv Higgins and told them, "We're gonna escort you two to the gallows so you can watch your pal hang. Maybe you'll decide you want to change your ways before you end up where Moxley's about to."

Clay and Higgins were handcuffed first, and then Moxley's hands were cuffed behind his back and he was led out of his cell. While Booker kept a firm grip on Moxley, Finkle ushered the other prisoners behind them, and Clay glanced at Higgins from the corner of his eye, wondering whether the man would clear him after Moxley's hanging.

Emerging from the jail into the early morning sun, the lawmen and their prisoners slogged through the street still muddy from the rain. A large crowd had gathered at the gallows, which was a skeletal affair built on skids, allowing it to be pulled from the alley behind the jail into the center of town when used. The hangman's noose swayed from the overhead beam in the morning breeze, and C. K. Moxley's knees suddenly seemed to be less than sturdy.

Clay and Higgins were some ten feet behind Moxley, and at the sight of the condemned killer, the crowd began to jeer and hiss. The procession was within twenty feet of the scaffold when galloping hooves sounded. Four riders abruptly charged into the crowd, scattering people and knocking several of them down, and the street was bedlam, with people screaming and shouting curses. Mike Moxley, gun in hand, led the charge of three other men and a saddled but riderless horse.

Aware that an attempt was being made to free Moxley, Booker and Finkle clawed for their guns, but the four horsemen opened fire first, cutting them down. The crowd immediately panicked and ran as fast as they could, while C. K. Moxley smiled at his brother as Mike dismounted and helped him onto the spare horse. Moxley flicked a glance at Mike's partners as they sent bullets at the feet of the scattering crowd, but the men were complete strangers.

Standing beside Higgins, who seemed frozen with fear and shock, Clay looked at the two lawmen lying in the mud. Booker was bleeding and moving slightly, but Finkle lay still, and the prisoner was sure the deputy was dead.

Moxley, his hands still cuffed behind him, called to his brother as Mike settled in his saddle, "Higgins is a traitor! Kill him!"

Without hesitation, Mike Moxley thumbed back the hammer of his revolver and shot Irv Higgins in the chest. When he fell, Mike shot him again. Then, spurring their horses, the outlaws galloped away. Clay Edwards stood watching the gang make good their escape until they had disappeared from sight. Then, dropping to his knees, he looked into the glazed eyes of Irv Higgins. "Don't die on me, Irv," he pleaded. "You're the only chance I have to prove I'm innocent."

The outlaws galloped across the hills, heading for the mountains. Breathing a sigh of relief, C. K. Moxley shouted up to his brother, leading his horse, "We need to get these cuffs off me! Otherwise I won't be able to ride fast enough!"

Smiling, Mike called back, "I already thought of that! Let's pull into that stand of trees up ahead and take care of it." Dismounting, Mike reached into his saddlebag and pulled out a hatchet he had stolen. Moxley grinned, scrambled off his mount, and lay on the wet ground, his arms out behind him. Mike positioned a rock under his brother's hands, lifted the hatchet, and with one blow cut the chain between the handcuffs, leaving Moxley wearing them like bracelets.

Remounting, they rode hard until their horses were exhausted. Pulling into a draw off the road that led into the Rockies over Monarch Pass, they slid from their mounts and walked them slowly around.

"Okay, Mike," said the outlaw leader, "tell me who your friends are—and how this came about."

Laughing, the younger Moxley stated, "Shake hands with Arnold Shumway, Vance Kebler, and Jeff Brodie." Mike then explained, "I watched the posse ride past the old shack where I was hidin', and I kept an eye out for their return. I wanted to see if they got you or not. I felt terrible when they came back with you and the others in tow—especially with Cook and Povey dead."

"They had it comin'," Moxley grunted. "They tried to run away, along with Higgins, even though I told 'em we needed to stick together. The posse cut 'em down in short order. That's why I told you to kill Higgins. The dirty rat was gonna take off on me."

Mike nodded. "Anyway, when my wound started to heal, I nosed around town quiet-like and learned about the trial date. I was in town the day of the trial, and when I heard people talkin' about your sentence, right then I made plans to come after you when they were leadin' you to the gallows." Gesturing at the new gang members, he continued, "I ran into these boys outside of town, and I could tell by the looks of 'em they were our kind. Told 'em we'd pay 'em good once we were back in business if they'd help me get you loose. They agreed . . . and here you are."

Setting his mud-colored eyes on the three drifters, Moxley grinned and said, "You bet we'll pay 'em good!"

"There is one thing that puzzles me, though," said Mike.

"What's that?"

"Wasn't that Clay Edwards who was taken to town with you and Higgins? And wasn't he watchin' at the gallows?"

Moxley laughed, slapping his legs. "Wait'll you hear this!" he exclaimed gleefully, and then he told his younger brother how Clay Edwards had become his substitute.

After hearing the tale, Mike roared appreciatively. "So you told 'em Edwards helped you rob the bank!"

"Yeah," Moxley confirmed, "and it worked! The judge gave him ten years in the penitentiary, same as he gave Higgins—for a crime he didn't commit!"

Back in town the doctor patched up Sheriff Art Booker's relatively slight shoulder wound, and then he performed surgery on an unconscious Irv Higgins, who barely clung to life. When the physician had done all that was possible for Higgins, he told Booker that two of his patients were about to have babies, and he needed to get to their ranches immediately. Higgins would have to be taken back to his cell and kept there, and the sheriff agreed, saying he would get a couple of men to carry the prisoner to the jail.

Clay Edwards was stretched out on his cot when Higgins was carried in and laid on a cot in the adjacent cell. Dismissing the bearers, Sheriff Booker stood over Higgins for a few moments, as if silently assessing his chances for survival. Then he left the cell and locked the door.

Standing and walking to the bars, Clay eyed the sling and asked, "Guess your wound wasn't too bad, eh, Sheriff?"

"Not as bad as Jay's," Booker replied flatly.

Clay nodded wordlessly. Then he commented, "Higgins doesn't look so good."

"He's in bad shape," confirmed Booker. "Doc had to leave town, so I had to bring Higgins here. You'll take the ride to Canon City tomorrow without him. If he lives, he'll make his trip later."

Clay watched the sheriff leave the cell area and close the door. With a sigh, he returned to his cot, sat down, and looked over at Higgins, lying so still just the other side of the bars that separated them.

Several hours had passed when Higgins finally began to stir. Heartened, Clay stood and went to the bars. Higgins looked up and met his gaze.

"Guess Moxley proved he was no friend of yours," the ex-gunfighter remarked dryly.

Higgins ran a tongue over his lips and whispered, "Yeah." He was silent for a long moment and then asked, "Doc say how . . . bad I am?"

Clay shook his head. "He probably told the sheriff, but I don't know."

"Moxley . . . Moxley got away, huh?"

"Yeah, I'm afraid so."

The outlaw's face filled with loathing. "Too bad. He deserves . . . to get what he gave me."

The rancher's pulse quickened. Now was his opportunity to talk Higgins into clearing him. He was about to speak when Higgins asked, "Could . . . could you get me some . . . water?"

Clay hurried to his own water pail and filled his tin cup. Reaching through the bars, he held the cup to Higgins's mouth and gave the wounded man a sip at a time. Pushing the cup away, the outlaw whispered, "I want revenge on Moxley, Edwards. Will you . . . get the sheriff . . . in here? There's somethin' . . . I gotta tell him."

"Sure thing," said Clay, his hope rising, "but will you tell him the truth about me, too?"

The wounded man nodded. "Sure," he mumbled. "No sense in you goin' to prison. I'd have . . . told it before, but you don't know C.K. He's . . . he's mean and brutal. I couldn't take the . . . chance."

"I understand," said Clay. Carrying the cup of water with him, he stepped to the cell door and shouted, "Sheriff! Sheriff!"

There was only silence.

He called repeatedly but soon realized that Booker had left the building. Turning back to Higgins, he knelt down beside the bars and gave him more water, saying, "The sheriff's gone."

"Look," Higgins said in a pained voice, "I ain't feelin' so good. If . . . if I give you some information, will you . . . pass it on to Booker?"

"Sure, but you're going to be all right. You've got to be," he said urgently. "You have to clear me."

"Listen," choked Higgins. "I know where Moxley . . . will go. He's got a cabin he uses for a hideout . . . high up in the Rockies near . . . near Buckskin Pass. You . . . you know where Buckskin Pass is?"

"I've heard of it," Clay replied. He wanted to shout at Higgins that he had to save his strength, that he had to live long enough to tell Booker the truth. But he merely asked, "It's a trail pass, isn't it? Not a road."

"Right. About ten miles west . . . of Aspen. Cabin's set deep in the trees . . . about five hundred feet below the timberline. Just off the trail that leads . . . over the pass. Moxley always . . . holes up there durin' the . . . coldest months. It's a good place to hide. I'm . . . sure he's gonna head—" Suddenly he spasmed, coughed, and gritted his teeth.

"Higgins!" gasped Clay, the pulse pounding in his temples. "Hang on! You've got to hang on!"

Higgins's lips moved soundlessly as he attempted to speak.

"Higgins!" Clay fairly screamed. "Who was the sixth man in the robbery?"

The dying man's body shook as he coughed and choked.

Clay dashed back to the cell door and bellowed, "Sheriff! Sheriff!"

Still no answer.

Kneeling beside Higgins again, he begged, "Come on. Tell me who the sixth man was! If I know that, I can still clear myself! Higgins! Higgins, please! Tell me!"

The outlaw's lips moved, but his voice was barely audible. Clay put his ear between the bars and heard him whisper, "Mike Moxley. It . . . was Moxley's . . . younger brother . . . Mike." Higgins's eyes rolled back in his head and his body went limp. He was dead.

The ex-gunfighter turned slowly and walked stiffly across his cell to his cot. Shoulders slumped, head bowed, he ran his fingers through his thick curly hair and tried to keep his despair at bay. Why did the sheriff have to be gone at just that time?

Standing, he paced back and forth in the small space, thinking about what Higgins had told him. Suddenly Clay decided to keep the information about Moxley's cabin and his brother to himself. There was only one alternative now. Somehow he had to escape—either while being transported to Canon City or after he was in the prison—and go after C. K. Moxley on his own. The gang leader would not tell the truth unless he was forced to do it . . . and Clay Edwards would be the one to do the forcing, no matter what it took.

Chapter Four

Wearing handcuffs on his wrists, having shackles on his ankles, and being well guarded, Clay Edwards had no means of escape during the four-day trip to Canon City. He bided his time, deciding that he would have to make his escape from the prison itself.

Arriving at the Colorado State Penitentiary, Clay was told that it was customary for each new prisoner to have a private interview with the tough and hard warden, Boyce Ruzek. After being clothed in prison grays, the innocent man was escorted to the warden's office by two uniformed, armed guards.

Ruzek was seated at his desk when Clay was ushered through the door, and the warden, a man in his late fifties with a squarely shaped body and face, looked up. The warden's thick, drooping gray mustache gave the impression that he was permanently scowling, and as Clay felt the man's gaze boring into him, he decided that Buzek's deep-set pale blue eyes looked like chunks of ice beneath the bushy gray brows. With his heavy jowls, a nose that looked as though it had been broken a number of times, and his stubbornly set face, the warden looked as tough as his reputation made him out to be.

Clay was led three feet from the desk and ordered to halt. Ruzek leaned back in his chair and stared silently and intently at his newest detainee for a painful ten seconds, then said stiffly, "So you're the famous Clay Edwards, the big, rough gunfighter!"

Ruzek let Clay stand there uncomfortably while he opened a humidor and pulled out a fat cigar. Then, with great deliberation, he closed the humidor, bit off and spit the end into a wastebasket beside his chair, struck a match, and lit the cigar. Puffing billows of smoke, he regarded the prisoner coldly and stated, "If you think being a famous gunfighter will give you privileges in here, Edwards, you're sadly mistaken. No doubt some of the inmates will fall at your feet when they learn who you are, 'cause in their eyes, you've got what it takes. You've got a big name."

"Sir," protested Clay, "I don't claim any—"

"You shut your trap, mister!" blared Ruzek, chewing on the cigar. "You don't speak until I say you can! Got that?"

"Yes, sir."

"Now, let me issue you a warning, gunslinger. We've got rules in this place—hard and fast rules. The guard who heads up your cell block will fill you in on them, and you better learn them quick. We don't coddle anyone in here, and if you break a rule, you pay. Understand?"

"Yes, sir," Clay replied, hating C. K. Moxley for putting him in such a horrible place.

Ruzek puffed on his cigar for a few moments, and then he asked gruffly, "Now, you got anything to say?"

"Just that you'll get no trouble from me," Clay replied. "I'm not guilty, and I'll be on good behavior because I want to get out of here as soon as possible."

Ruzek grinned sardonically, and then he laughed. "Not guilty, eh? Yeah, that's what they all say!" He motioned to the guards. "Take him away, fellas."

The guards wheeled Clay around and propelled him toward the door. Suddenly the warden said sharply, "Edwards!"

Clay looked over his shoulder and waited for the man to go on.

"I don't like gunfighters. And if you cause me any trouble, you'll be dealt with twice as hard as any other convict. Do I make myself clear?"

"Yes, sir," said Clay, doubling his determination to break out of the place.

Word spread quickly through the prison that the famous gunfighter Clay Edwards was now an inmate, and during meals and free time in the exercise yard men approached him and asked numerous questions about his life. On the third day, when he was eating breakfast in the mess hall, he was sitting between his cellmate and a convict who occupied an adjacent cell. While sipping his coffee, Clay noticed a mountain of a man glaring at him from two tables away. Their eyes met and held briefly, and then Clay looked away. Turning to his cellmate, he asked, "Who's the ugly, bald giant?"

"Name's Garth Candler," Tom Taylor replied. "Why?"

"He's giving me the evil eye."

"Don't mess with him," Taylor warned. "He's as mean as he's ugly, and that huge body of his is rock hard—which he likes to prove any chance he gets. He's doing a life sentence for murder with no possibility of parole. So are those two brutes with him, Abe Willard and Eugene Hudson. Candler's the boss in this place, and most everybody wants to be his friend. It's safer that way. If he don't like you, he'll find a way to hurt you when the guards ain't lookin'. Just stay clear of him."

Clay nodded, and as he drank his coffee, he let his eyes drift back to the massive convict. As bald as a cue ball, Garth Candler wore a thick black mustache that matched his heavy eyebrows. He had huge sloping shoulders, a neck like a tree stump, and upper arms so muscular that they looked as though the slightest flex would split the sleeves of his gray prison shirt. Apparently feeling Clay's gaze, Candler broke off talking to the man beside him and stared again at the newcomer. The look in the giant's eyes was hostile, but as Clay was not the kind to back down from anybody, he met the hostile gaze with one of defiance. Candler grinned malevolently and then looked away.

Clay was assigned to a work detail that day, breaking large rocks into gravel with a sledgehammer. After eight grueling hours of swinging the hammer, the prisoners were released into the exercise yard. The ex-gunfighter was milling about with several other men when Garth Candler lumbered toward him with his friends flanking him. He glared at Clay, regarding him coldly, and then the huge man growled, "I know about you, Edwards. You're the skunk who gunned down Kelley Byars up in Denver. Well, he was my best friend—and I'm gonna fix you!"

Showing no fear in spite of the man's intimidating size and mien, Clay retorted evenly, "I killed Byars because he challenged me. It was a fair fight, and anyone who saw it would agree."

Candler snarled, "Don't make no difference what you say, Edwards. You gunned down my best friend. I'd kill you right here and now if I thought I could get away with it, but it ain't worth the chance. It especially ain't worth goin' to the hole over. But I'm gonna fix you good. You wait and see."

Ignoring the threat, Clay turned and walked away.

The next afternoon, after the work detail was finished, the convicts once again stood around the exercise yard. Big Garth Candler leaned against the building and eyed Clay Edwards across the yard. Turning to the dozen or so men who stood with him, Candler ordered, "You guys stay real close, 'cause I'm gonna put on a show and I want all of you to back up whatever I say. Got it?"

The group nodded that they understood.

Looking at Abe Willard and Eugene Hudson, Candler said, "Here's my plan: I'm gonna start an argument with Edwards, and you men shove him into me real hard once things get heated up. I'll go down, makin' it look like he punched me. That's all it'll take to convince them stupid guards that he started it. He'll get three months in the hole—three months of misery for Kelley Byars's killer." He chuckled, adding, "But don't call for the guards too soon. I want to squeeze Edwards some before the scuffle's stopped."

Candler pushed himself away from the building and sauntered over to Clay. Keeping his voice low so as not to arouse the guards keeping watch on the wall, the giant stepped close and said, "I've been thinkin' about what you did to my friend. Seems to me you could've tried to talk him out of drawing against you."

"I did try to talk him out of it!" Clay countered, clearly irritated. "Your friend was just a wet-nosed green-horn wanting to become famous for taking me out in a quick-draw. That's the long and the short of it, and I don't want to hear any more about it. Go on about your business, Candler!"

Clay's loud, angry retort was the cue for Willard and Hudson, who stood unnoticed behind him. Suddenly they shoved him hard against Candler, and the big man hit the ground as if he had been punched. Inmates all over the yard turned and watched when Willard snarled at Clay, "You dirty scum! You slugged my friend! He didn't do nothin' to you!"

While Candler rose to his feet, Clay yelled at Willard, "I didn't touch him, and you know it!"

"I'll fight my own battles!" Candler snarled as he steadied himself. "Nobody punches me and gets away with it!" As he spoke, he spun Clay around so that he was behind him, and he ran his hands under his arms, locking him in a bear hug. Lifting his adversary off his feet, Candler squeezed so hard that Clay's ribs almost popped.

As the guards on the wall began looking down at the ruckus, Eugene Hudson cupped his hands to his mouth and shouted, "Guards, hurry! The gunfighter's beatin' up Garth!"

Tan-uniformed men scrambled down from the wall

while others plunged out the doors of the main building, all of them in a rush to break up the fight. Candler's men shouted at the oncoming guards that Clay had attacked the huge inmate, and though the other convicts in the yard knew immediately what had happened, they feared the giant and his cronies and would not interfere or speak the truth.

Feeling his breath being squeezed out of him, Clay struggled to fight back. He was also infuriated by Candler's dirty tactics, which gave him added resolve. Having been in more fights than he could count, and being an old hand at battling men bigger than he, he threw his hands back at Candler's face, extending his thumbs. A finger jabbed in the eye was one of the best ways to make a man let go.

Clay felt the giant's right eyeball split as he rammed his thumb into it. Candler screamed shrilly and released the smaller man just as the guards came rushing up. Hearing the babel of voices insisting that Clay had started the fight, the guards seized the new inmate and dragged him from the yard. Candler, hollering that he was blind, was rushed to the infirmary as he held his hand over his eye while blood oozed between his fingers.

Warden Boyce Ruzek was waiting in front of his desk, his arms crossed, when the four guards hauled Clay into the office and stood him before the warden. They quickly told Ruzek that according to a number of inmates, Clay had attacked Candler.

While the guards held Clay tight, the warden glared at him and snapped, "I warned you to watch your step, mister! But you didn't, and now you're going to pay for your offense! Normally you'd get three months in the hole for starting a fight, but seeing as how you think you're above the rules here, you're going in for six!" He glanced at the guards and ordered, "Take him away!"

Clay tried to explain the truth to Ruzek as the guards led him from the office, but the warden turned a deaf ear.

The solitary cell, known as the hole, was a small,

six-by-eight cubicle with no chair and only a straw mat to sleep on. It had a damp dirt floor and stone walls, and it was infested with insects and vermin. The single, solid door was made of half-inch pig iron, and the cell's only window was the size of a cigar box and too high off the floor to see anything but sky. The man confined in solitary was given the same three meals a day as the rest of the inmates, but his slop jar was emptied only once a week, so the stench of the hole was rank. He was allowed a "spit" bath with half a gallon of water once a week, but no shaves and no haircuts were given.

When the door of the dreadful cell was slammed shut and locked behind him on May 26, 1884, Clay Edwards burned with hatred toward C. K. Moxley for putting him in prison, and toward Garth Candler for putting him in solitary.

The days passed slowly in the gloomy cell, but Clay worked hard at maintaining both his sanity and his body, exercising by doing push-ups and running in place. As much as possible he ignored the horrendous stench, the dampness, the dim light, and the tiny creatures that roamed the walls and the earthen floor. He constantly dreamed of the day he would escape and go after Moxley, and it was his determination to find the outlaw that kept his spirit from breaking.

On November 26, 1884, a cold, snowy day, Clay Edwards was released from solitary, harboring a deep bitterness toward Garth Candler and a burning hatred for C. K. Moxley. He was permitted a hot bath and then given a haircut by the prison barber and allowed to shave. Wearing clean prison grays and flanked by two guards, he was ushered into Warden Boyce Ruzek's office. Ruzek was seated behind his desk, chewing on a dead cigar, and he kept the prisoner waiting for several long minutes before he looked up. Sneering, he asked sarcastically, "Well, did you enjoy your stay in the hole?"

Clay's expression was grim and his voice was toneless as he replied, "You know the answer to that . . . sir."

Leaning back in his chair, Ruzek regarded the inmate sternly, and then he stated, "Let me warn you, Edwards. If you get into trouble again, you'll go back to solitary—for a year this time."

"I can tell you right now, sir," Clay said, "that Garth Candler will no doubt pull the same maneuver to put me back in the hole. He set me up last time, and I'm sure he'll do it again."

Ruzek sniffed derisively. "You know you permanently blinded Candler in one eye. But don't worry. He won't cause you any more trouble. You see, he and two of his pals escaped from here almost three months ago and have never been caught. So let's see if you can stay out of trouble now. The guards will show you to your new cell."

Clay was led to a cell occupied by a dark-haired man in his early thirties. When the guards opened the door, one of them declared, "Got a cellmate for you, Framm. He was in solitary when you came here, but I'm sure you've heard about him. Name's Clay Edwards."

"You bet I have," the convict exclaimed incredulously as he rose from his cot. "In fact I heard about him long before I ever saw this stinkin' prison." Extending his right hand to Clay, he said, "I'm Nick Framm."

While Clay shook the man's hand, the guard explained, "Framm's in for life for murdering a total of seven people . . . men and women." The guard looked disparagingly from one man to the other. "Gunslingers and murderers—guess you're all the same. You two oughtta get along famously."

Framm waited until the guards were gone, then said, "I'm really glad to make your acquaintance, and any man who can use a gun like you is a pal of mine. Matter of fact, I knew one guy you killed. Dobie Rhodes. Remember him?"

Clay sat down on the unoccupied cot. "Yeah. I shot it out with him in Cheyenne."

"Sure enough. He was one fast shooter"—Framm laughed dryly—"but obviously you were faster. I heard all about it from a pal of mine in Cheyenne. Rhodes and I had a bit of a fuss over cards in Laramie City about a month before you sent him to his just reward. Cheated me, he did. Only I ain't no gunslick, so I didn't accuse him. I do my killin' from behind, so's I know I'm the one's gonna come out alive. No leather slappin' for me. Sure am glad you killed him, though. I also heard about you outdrawin' Mack Dinsmore over in Colorado City—oh, yeah, and Tex Hall in that little Kansas town . . . what is it?"

Reluctantly Clay answered, "Sargent."

"Yeah, Sargent, that was it. Those guys were known to be pretty good. But you're better, of course."

Clay stretched out on the cot and folded his hands behind his head, saying nothing.

Still on his feet, Framm paced slowly back and forth. Clearly assuming that the two of them were like-minded, he snorted, "That guard don't know the half of it. Actually, I've murdered twelve people. Guns, knives—I even drowned one woman in her washtub. Ah, that was fun! All of 'em were fun, but that was the best. She really put up a fight. Some thrill, ain't it? Snuffin' out a human life, I mean. It's . . . it's almost like bein' a god of some kind, havin' that kind of power of life and death."

The man made Clay's skin crawl. Looking up at him from the cot, he asked, "Since the law knows about you killing so many people, how did you escape being hanged?"

Framm threw his head back, laughed, and replied, "It was pure good luck, it was! The judge I went before after bein' caught had once sent an innocent man to the gallows. I heard about it from the guy in the next cell. Seems when the judge learned the hanged man was innocent, it gave him such nightmares that ever since it happened, he's given life sentences to men convicted of murder. He refuses to hang 'em."

"You sure were fortunate," Clay agreed.

Framm stopped pacing and stood over Clay. "How come you're in here?" he asked.

Sighing, Clay sat up, leaned his back against the wall, and explained how he was framed by C. K. Moxley.

When Clay had finished, Framm smacked his fist into his palm and declared, "You oughtta bust outta here and go after him!"

"I've had six months to think about it," Clay remarked, "and I know that the only way I can clear myself is to do just that. I've got to get my hands on Moxley and force him to tell the truth to the law."

Shaking his head, the murderer mused, "Yeah, but it might take you a long time to find him. Who knows where he is by now."

"As a matter of fact, I do. One of his cronies told me where he hides out during the winter months. If I could break out of here now, I could get to him, hog-tie the lying snake, drag him to the nearest lawman, and make him confess to framing me."

Framm stepped to the cell door and looked into the narrow corridor, making sure there was no one close enough to hear them. Sitting down beside Clay on the cot, he asked quietly, "You really want to bust outta here?"

"You bet. I've been working on a scheme or two."

"Well, you can forget your schemes. I've got a ticket outta here in just three days. You can come with me if you want. Matter of fact, I'll go with you and help you capture Moxley, 'cause once you're cleared, I want to see you facin' men in gunfights." He chuckled. "It'd be a real thrill to watch you cut 'em down."

Clay would not jeopardize his escape by telling Nick Framm he had hung up his gun. Letting him think things would go as Framm had just described them, he said, "How are you going to escape?"

"I guess you know about Garth Candler, Abe Willard, and Eugene Hudson escapin'."

"Yeah. The warden told me Candler and two of his

pals broke out. He didn't say how they made good their escape, though."

Framm smiled. "That's 'cause he don't know . . . but I do. One of the guards helped 'em. A guy named Fred Scudder. Candler had some money stashed, bidin' his time till he found a guard he thought he could trust—or I should say, one crooked enough. Anyway, he gave the money to Scudder, and the guard let 'em out, makin' it look like a genuine break."

"How do you know all that?"

Grinning triumphantly, the murderer said, "I got my hands on a note that was passed between Scudder and Candler. Scudder's handwritin' is real odd, makin' it easy to identify—so I just pulled me a little blackmail. Told Scudder I have the note—I quoted it to him so's he'd know I wasn't kiddin'—and I told him I'd give the note to Ruzek if he didn't get me outta here right away." Framm laughed, adding, "He fixed it up immediately."

"So how's it going to work?"

"About four months ago the prison's well started puttin' out polluted water. You know about it?"

"No. They don't tell you anything when you're in the hole."

"Well, ever since then they've had to cart the water in here from outside. Every five days a wagon bearin' a large water tank is brought in, and the empty tank it replaces is taken out. The empty one's already waitin' on another wagon so's the full one can be immediately hooked up. Anyway, the openin' at the top of the tank is large enough for a man to crawl inside. Scudder will be drivin' the empty one out, and it's all set for me to be inside the empty tank when it goes in three days." The convict shrugged. "It's big enough for two men, so there's no reason why you can't go with me."

"How do you know you can trust Scudder?" queried Clay. "Maybe he'll just pretend to be letting you out but then put a gun on you and demand the note. Once you give it to him, he can slam you right back in here and even say he caught you trying to escape."

Framm tapped his temple. "Brains, my friend! I got brains! I mailed the note to a buddy of mine on the outside. If he don't hear from me inside a week's time, he's got instructions to get it to Ruzek immediately—and Scudder's goose'd be cooked." He laughed again. "I told Scudder about it, and he was madder'n a wet hen, but he ain't gonna pull nothin' on me, I can guarantee you that."

Nodding appreciatively, Clay remarked, "You're a sharp one, Nick, I'll say that for you."

"You got that right. And once we're outside these walls, you and me are long gone."

"That is, if we can stay ahead of the law," Clay said, chuckling humorlessly.

"It'll be a cinch," Framm responded. "There ain't enough lawmen in these parts to spend time trackin' escaped convicts. That's why Garth Candler and his pals have never been caught. The guards gave chase for a few hours, but they had to return to their duties here at the prison without 'em. Sometimes the authorities'll send a U.S. marshal after an escapee, but usually if the guards fail to catch the convict, he'll get away."

"Good!" exclaimed Clay, feeling hopeful. "Then all I need is to get away clean and make it to Buckskin Pass. Once I've got C.K. Moxley in my clutches, I'll make him tell the truth, and the law won't want me anymore."

Nick Framm nodded as he walked to a small table beside his cot. Opening a tin of tobacco, he rolled a cigarette and lit it, and as he blew smoke toward the ceiling, he looked at Clay with a strange glint in his eyes. "I'll let you in on somethin' I've got planned. I'm gonna kill me four people—three of 'em are the men who turned me in to the law when they saw me murder a farmer, and the other is that town marshal who arrested me. You can help me if you want to."

Horrified at the thought—though careful not to let on how he felt—Clay shook his head and laughed hollowly. "I wouldn't want to deprive you of all the revenge you've got coming, Nick. I'll let you take care of them."

Later that afternoon, while the prisoners were walking around the snow-covered exercise yard, Clay Edwards noticed his cellmate talking to a guard. During supper, Framm sat beside Clay and whispered that he had talked to Fred Scudder and it was all set: They would be assigned to help with the exchanging of the water tanks, and Scudder would distract the other guards so Framm and Clay could climb into the empty tank. In just three days Clay could begin the hunt for C. K. Moxley.

Clay Edwards and Nick Framm felt the wagon draw to a halt. A few moments later they heard the muffled call of the guard: "Okay, Framm! It's clear!"

Opening the wooden lid in the top of the round tank, Framm cautiously stuck his head out. Then he threw open the lid and crawled out, with Clay immediately behind him. Snow was lightly falling from a gray sky, and the two escaped convicts hopped from the wagon onto the ground that already had a deep covering of snow. The murderer pulled his prison-issue coat tight around him and looked up at the guard, saying sarcastically, "You done real good, Scudder. I thank you kindly."

"Keep your thanks, Framm," snarled Scudder from the wagon seat. "And just don't expect it to be too long till someone discovers you're gone. They'll probably be after you before I even get back to the prison."

"We can handle that," Framm declared cockily. Turning to Clay, he said, "Come on, let's hightail it outta here!"

Running hard, the two escapees headed northwest toward Parkdale, some ten miles away, where they planned to cross the Currant River that night—after breaking into a clothing store and donning new clothes. Just before they reached the dense forest, Clay looked back at the somber prison in the distance. Elated at having his freedom, he ran with renewed energy, though he knew he would have to do something about Nick Framm. He could not allow the man to murder more people.

When they were deep in the timber, they paused to catch their breath. The snow was coming down harder and the temperature was dropping. "We gotta get horses," panted Framm.

Clay nodded wordlessly, looking around. Then he pointed through the trees off to their left. "Look! There's a small farm over there," he said breathlessly. "Horses in the corral by the barn."

The farm buildings were at the edge of the woods about a hundred yards from where the men stood. Waiting till their breathing was back to normal, they then hurried toward the place, halting about fifty feet back in the shelter of the trees. They looked carefully all around, but no one was in sight. "Okay," said Framm. "Let's make a dash for the barn and find us some saddles and bridles."

Framm had apparently sensed Clay's move at him a fraction of a second before it happened, for he suddenly turned. But it was too late to dodge the rock-hard fist that met his jaw. The murderer went down, unconscious. Clay made sure Framm was out completely, then ran as fast as he could to the barn. Plunging inside, he soon found what he had hoped to, and he dashed back to Framm, holding a length of rope.

Framm came to and found himself tied securely to an aspen tree, his hands and feet trussed up tight. He lifted his glassy eyes to Clay, who was standing a few feet away, brushing snow from his curly hair. Swearing, the murdered demanded, "What do you think you're doin', Edwards? I got you outta that stinkin' prison! Is this any way to treat me?"

"I sure do appreciate your getting me out, Framm," Clay replied, "but I can't let you murder anyone else. The guards'll be along shortly, I'm sure, to take you back—and hopefully keep you where you belong."

An angry, mottled flush rose on Framm's cheeks. His

eyes were wild as he yelled, "You dirty scum! I'll break out again and I'll come after you and kill you! I swear it! I'll kill you!"

"That's a chance I'll have to take," Clay retorted calmly.

Half insane with fury, Framm screamed, "I'll tell the warden you're goin' to Buckskin Pass, and they'll trail you in no time! If I can't break out, I'll kill you when they put you back in prison!"

"By the time the law can catch up to me, I'll have Moxley in my hands," the ex-gunfighter stated. "If I have to make him write it in his own blood, he's going to clear me." He then shook his head and knelt beside Framm. "I sure can't have your screams arousing someone in the farmhouse." As he spoke he sent another powerful blow to Framm's jaw, again knocking him out, and then he took out his handkerchief and gagged the escaped convict.

Minutes later Clay Edwards rode toward Parkdale on a stolen horse. Though it went against his grain to steal, he had no choice. He had to get to Buckskin Pass as soon as possible.

Chapter Five

That same November morning, at a house in Canon City, beautiful Barbara LaBonde stirred beneath the covers, rolled over in her bed, and opened her eyes. She swept back her black hair from her face and gingerly touched the hollow of her left jaw. It was still swollen. Throwing off the covers, Barbara rose and dangled her feet over the edge of the bed. She sat there for a few seconds then stood and crossed the room to her dressing table and sat on the padded bench.

Looking at her weary twenty-five-year-old face in the mirror, she was pleased that at least some of the swelling had finally gone down from the beating her husband had given her two days before. Her face had been so badly swollen that her sky-blue eyes had been mere slits. However, many of the purple and yellow bruises were still stark and quite visible, and she would probably have them for at least another week.

Picking up her hairbrush, Barbara ran it repeatedly through her hair until it was fluffy and lay on her shoulders in soft swirls. She then rose from the bench and picked up her robe from the back of a chair. Slipping into it, she left the bedroom and headed for the kitchen, but she abruptly stopped as she reached the adjoining bedroom.

Her husband, Jack, was asleep on the bed, fully clothed and snoring loudly. He reeked from whiskey, and his shirt was smeared with rouge and lip paint, as was his face. Eyeing him bitterly, Barbara shook her head in disgust, telling herself that if she had needed a reminder of why she took off her wedding ring three days ago, she did not need one any longer. Closing the door, she walked briskly to the kitchen.

A half hour later the lovely brunette was eating breakfast when she heard shuffling feet in the hallway. She looked up as her husband, droopy-eyed, groped his way into the kitchen. Anger danced in her eyes as she regarded him with loathing and aversion.

Jack leaned against the cupboard and met her fiery gaze. "You don't have to look at me like that," he said with a thick tongue.

"Just how am I supposed to look at you?" she snapped tartly. "I didn't expect to see you inside this house again."

Ignoring her reply, Jack LaBonde stumbled to the table and held onto it to keep from falling, asking, "Where's my breakfast?"

"There is none!"

"Well, why not?" he pressed, running his hand over his face and then through his tousled hair.

Barbara retorted, "Because you don't live here anymore, remember? It's all over between us! This marriage—which was never a marriage from its first day—is over!"

Jack dropped into a chair across the table from his wife, whining, "Aw, now, honey. This is ridiculous. You still love me, I know you do."

"Don't you honey me—and I can't stand the sight of you!" she countered. "I'm sick of your drinking, I'm through forgiving you for your womanizing, and I'm not taking any more beatings! You're not a husband! You're nothing but a drunken, lustful cad!"

Running a shaky palm over his flushed face, Jack mumbled, "Now, honey, you don't mean that. You're just a little upset because—"

"I do too mean it!" Barbara shouted, rising to her feet. "No more, Jack! You agreed to move out yesterday. Now, go on and get out of this house!"

Jack seemed to become smaller before her eyes. Tears filled his bloodshot eyes, and his lower lip began to quiver. Sniffing, he begged, "Just one more chance, Barbara, please! Just give me one more chance!"

Barbara's glare was hard. Having no compassion for the man, she railed at him, "Look at you! Your hair looks like a rat's nest, your eyes are bloodshot from whiskey, and there's rouge and lip paint on your shirt! What woman were you with last night? You're a disgrace, Jack! You're just like my father and my brothers. You're not worth the cost of the bullet it would take to put you out of your misery! Get out, Jack! Get out!"

Suddenly suffused with anger, Jack LaBonde stood up and shook his fist at her, bellowing, "I'll beat you to death, woman!" He then swung, but Barbara leapt out of the way. Swearing, Jack stumbled after her, but she dashed into the hallway, ran into the back bedroom, and locked the door.

Bracing her back against the door, Barbara heard Jack cursing as he approached. Once down the hall, he pounded on the door while twisting the knob, demanding that she open it. After nearly five minutes he gave up, and mumbling incoherently, his shuffling footsteps retreated. The front door of the house banged open, and Barbara hurried to a window and saw him heading across the yard toward the street. "Yeah, that's it," she said aloud. "Back to the good old Rusty Lantern, Jack. Your women and your whiskey are there. That's where you belong."

Barbara told herself that she had to get away from Canon City before Jack did finally beat her to death. She would take what belongings she could pack in a suitcase, catch the next stagecoach north, and go to her sister's home in Aspen. Susan had told her many times to leave Jack and come live with her. Putting her fingers to her temples, Barbara tried to remember what day of the week it was. "It's Tuesday!" she exclaimed. "The stage comes through here today!"

It was almost eleven-thirty when Barbara LaBonde,

carrying her suitcase, trudged through the snow to Main Street. The snow was falling harder as she made her way toward the Wells Fargo office, the stagecoach and horses parked in front covered with a layer of snow.

Stepping through the door of the office, Barbara brushed the snowflakes from her hat and shoulders and set her suitcase down. Agent Don Wise was standing next to the stove, talking to the driver and shotgunner.

"Good mornin', ma'am," said Wise, a sandy-haired man of thirty. "You're Mrs. LaBonde, aren't you? How can I help you?"

"You're correct, I am Mrs. LaBonde, and I'd like passage on the stage going north to Aspen," Barbara replied with a smile, pulling off her gloves.

"Well, you're in luck. We've got one seat available. You're also lucky that you've chosen today to travel, 'cause this is the last stage to head north into the Rockies till spring."

"Oh?"

"Yes, ma'am. Stagecoaches aren't able to navigate through the deep snows that'll be hitting soon." The agent then gestured to the men and said, "This here's Claude Overstreet, he's driving the stage you saw outside, and this is Bill Mundy, the shotgun guard." Overstreet was in his late fifties and of medium height and build, although his hands, shoulders, and arms spoke of considerable strength. Mundy was about the same size, but in his early thirties.

Both men touched their hat brims and smiled, though their gazes strayed to the bruises on Barbara's face.

Not meeting their eyes and turning her face slightly, hoping to obscure their view, the brunette murmured, "A pleasure, gentlemen."

Wise stepped behind the counter and said, "Ma'am, before I take your money, I feel obliged to warn you that the Utes have been on the rampage of late. They wiped out a small wagon train near Buena Vista four days ago, and as this stage goes right through their territory, this trip could be dangerous."

Eager to get away from her brutal husband, who she felt could be equally dangerous, she remarked, "Apparently your other passengers are willing to take the chance. I'll take it, too."

"Yes, ma'am," said the agent, pulling a ticket from the drawer.

While she was paying, Barbara asked, "Are any of the other passengers from Canon City?"

"No, ma'am," Wise replied. "Everybody else came from Pueblo. That's where this stage originates."

Barbara nodded silently, placing the change in her purse. At that moment the other passengers returned from the café where they had eaten an early lunch. While Overstreet and Mundy took Barbara's suitcase out to the stage, the travelers filed into the office and stomped the snow off their boots, closing the door behind them.

Don Wise told the other passengers that the brunette would be joining them, and they began to introduce themselves. Two elderly women, both small-boned and thin, gave their names as Mattie Phelps and Martha Bowman. Also traveling together were a pair of teenage boys. Jim McLaughlin was tall, dark, and eighteen, while Leonard Robertson was of medium height, blond, and seventeen. Barbara was surprised that both boys were wearing sidearms. The fifth passenger was a tall, stocky, muscular blond man in his mid-thirties. Barbara did not like the hint of a leer in his eyes as he introduced himself as Gene Fletcher.

Light snow was still falling as the passengers boarded the coach a few minutes later. Barbara took a window seat, and Gene Fletcher made an obvious switch at the last moment, seating himself directly across from the beautiful brunette—a move that did not escape Barbara's notice. The elderly women sat facing each other in the middle of the seats, while the youths each took the window seats on the opposite side of the coach.

The stage pulled away from the Wells Fargo office at exactly twelve noon, and as it passed the Rusty Lantern

Saloon, Barbara cast a quick glance toward the door, knowing Jack was inside drinking himself into a stupor, with some painted hussy clinging to him. She asked herself why she had ever thought she loved the man in the first place but then decided it did not matter. Whatever she had felt for Jack LaBonde, he had managed to kill it.

Canon City had hardly passed from view when Mattie Phelps, who sat next to Fletcher, said, "Where are you bound, Mrs. LaBonde?"

"Aspen," Barbara replied with a smile.

"Oh. I've heard it's a nice place. Is that where you're from?"

Barbara saw the woman studying her swollen and bruised face, and she was certain that what she really wanted to know was how it happened. "No, ma'am," replied the brunette. "But I'm moving there. My older sister lives there."

"That's nice," Mattie remarked, nodding. "I'm going to visit my granddaughter and her family in Buena Vista." Indicating the woman across from her, Mattie added, "Martha will be getting off at our next swing station, which is a few miles past Parkdale. She's going to visit her son and his family for the winter."

Barbara merely nodded. Feeling Fletcher's pale blue eyes on her, she fleetingly glanced at him and then looked away. The young men were looking over at her, but there was only innocence in their eyes. She smiled and they both smiled in return.

They rode along in silence for a while. The snow pelted the north side of the stage, and Jim McLaughlin quickly dropped the leather curtains on the windows. Buffalo-hide blankets covered the legs of the passengers, and the elderly women pulled them up close to their faces.

Gene Fletcher broke the silence by saying, "I believe the agent in Canon City called you Mrs. LaBonde. However, I noticed before you put your gloves on that you're not wearing a wedding ring. You a widow?"

Regarding him icily, Barbara's face flushed as she replied crisply, "No."

"Divorced?"

"Not yet. However, that is my business—and I would appreciate your minding your own business."

Fletcher flushed angrily, but then mumbled, "Sorry. I didn't mean to rile you. I just thought if you were unattached, you and I might get to know each other better. See, I'm going to Fairplay, and if we became good friends on the trip, it wouldn't be any trouble at all for me to ride a horse back over to Aspen at any time. Maybe we could, you know . . ."

Barbara's eyes were as cold as ice—as was her voice. "Look, Mr. Fletcher, I'm not interested in you or anybody like you! Please leave me alone."

Fletcher raised his eyebrows and whistled softly. "That's what I like in a woman. A little fire."

"Why don't you do as the lady asked, Mr. Fletcher, and leave her alone?" young Jim McLaughlin spoke up.

Leaning across the coach and shaking his finger at the youth, Fletcher hissed, "You butt out, kid! If I want to talk to the lady, I'll do so! Keep your nose out from where it doesn't belong!"

His voice low and level, Jim stated, "Mrs. LaBonde asked you to leave her alone, sir. It seems to me you should honor her request. Is that so unreasonable?"

Everyone's eyes were on Fletcher. He glared at the youth for a moment, then settled back in his seat, and the tension that had built up eased. Barbara looked at Jim and gave him a warm smile. "You're a nice young man," she said softly. "Thank you for your kindness."

Jim grinned, glanced at his friend, then stared at the floor.

Barbara watched the falling snow for a few minutes, but she could feel Gene Fletcher's eyes on her. For several minutes she held her gaze out the window, but finally she succumbed and looked at him. He gave her a lecherous grin, and her immediate rage suffused her bruised cheeks with florid color. She glared at him, burning him with loathing from steady, unblinking eyes. Finally he looked away and stared out the window himself.

The six horses labored up a steep grade, the coach sandwiched between the snow-covered shoulders of the mountain road. The wind was howling through the pines, coating the vehicle with freezing white snow. The passengers were forced to drop the leather curtains on the other side, throwing the interior into a deep gloom.

Barbara LaBonde tugged at the buffalo-hide blanket, pulling it up to her chin. She thought of Jack and all the misery he had dealt her, and then her mind slipped further back—to a father who had treated her mother in a like manner. Her childhood had been one of anguish, sorrow, and terror, living in a home where her drunken father continuously beat her mother, two brothers, sister, and her, and she had lost track of how many times her mother had forgiven the man for his illicit affairs with women. Disappointment had been added to misery when her brothers grew up, married, and turned out to be exactly like their father.

Barbara clenched her teeth and stared down at the floor. With an intense dislike for men in general, she told herself she would not trust another man as far as she could throw Pike's Peak.

Clay Edwards pushed the stolen horse through the wind-whipped snow, holding a northwest course as best he could. Despite the difficulty it made for traveling, he was glad it was snowing, for the guards had undoubtedly caught up with Nick Framm and he had certainly told them where he was headed. But even if the snow did not convince them to give up their pursuit sooner than they normally would, the drifting, blowing snow would quickly cover his tracks.

Being unfamiliar with the territory, he was not always sure he was heading in the proper direction. He had been riding for nearly an hour when he topped a rise and looked back. About a quarter mile below were four riders, vague and indistinct in the swirling snow. Then the wind ceased for a moment, and with it the blowing snow, and he could make out the tan overcoats and hats of the prison guards. His heart beat faster. The guards must have been even closer than he had thought when he left Framm.

At the same time Clay spotted the guards, they spotted him. One of them shouted and pointed his way, and they instantly put their horses to a trot and headed toward him.

The escapee spurred his horse, making it climb as fast as possible. Leaving the path to find a place to hide, he guided the animal into a deep forest where the ground leveled off. The tree limbs lashed at his face, stinging him mercilessly, but he pressed on for several minutes. Suddenly he came out of the timber into a clearing and found himself staring at a sheer rock wall that was studded with brush and rose some eighty feet.

Panicking, Clay looked all around and realized that because of the density of the forest, he had not been aware that he was heading into a box canyon. The towering walls loomed over him on three sides. There was no direction to go except back the way he had come . . . or straight up.

He could hear the guards shouting. They had found his trail through the trees and were coming on fast. They would be on him any minute. His heart pumped madly, and his quick, short, breaths emerged in frosty clouds on the frigid air. He was going to have to leave the horse and take the only way out.

Leaping from the saddle, he made a dash for the north face of the canyon. The clumps of brush that grew out of its cracked and pitted surface were coated with snow. Grasping limbs, he started climbing, reaching from one clump to another. He was about fifteen feet up when his foot slipped and he lost his hold, falling ten feet to a large clump of shrub. Able to grab one of its thick limbs, he gasped for breath and listened to the guards getting closer.

Drawing on reserves of strength, Clay resumed his difficult and dangerous climb. The bone-chilling wind whipped across the frozen face of the cliff and across the escapee's face as well. When he heard the shouts from below, Clay knew without looking that the guards had ridden into the clearing and spotted him.

He kept climbing.

"Edwards!" came a voice clearly. "Halt, or we'll shoot!"

Clay's breath was sawing in and out of his lungs. His arms and legs felt as though they were weighted down with lead, but he continued on. He could see the rim of the cliff looming above him, not more than twenty-five feet away. Determined to make it, he reached up, grabbed the next bush, and painfully yet methodically pulled himself up to it, then took hold of the next one.

"Edwards!" came the voice again, above the whine of the icy wind. "I'm giving you one more chance to surrender! Come down now!"

Cold as it was, Clay could feel sweat running down the middle of his back. If he could only make it to the top . . .

The crack of a rifle fractured the mountain air. At the same instant a bullet whacked into the rock less than a foot from the fleeing man's head, shattering fragments and ricocheting away. Clay paused, gripping his precarious handholds, and looked down. Three of the guards had their rifles shouldered and aimed at him. The fourth was levering a fresh cartridge into his weapon.

They waited to see what he was going to do.

Panting hard, Clay thought of the solitary cell at the prison—and of Boyce Ruzek. If he surrendered, the hard-nosed warden would certainly toss him into the hole and throw away the key. He decided he would rather be dead. He would take the gamble. The lip of the cliff was now within twenty feet. If he could make it over the edge, he had a good chance of eluding capture. It would take the guards quite a while to ride back out of the canyon and around the shoulder of the mountain. By that time, even on foot, he could find a hiding place and wait them out.

Summoning strength from unknown resources, impelled by memories of the hole, Clay Edwards resumed his daring climb. As he did, he heard one of the guards swear and shout, "Shoot him! Shoot him!"

Clay crawled upward hand over hand, digging his toes into whatever would support them. A barrage of gunfire exploded from below, and lead chewed into the rock all around him, whining angrily as it flew off the hard surface.

Never had he experienced such complete and extreme soul-rending desperation. His scalp tingled and his heart thundered in his breast like a trapped animal as he scurried for safety.

Bullets continued to fly, and he felt one rip through the coat sleeve on his right arm while another buzzed past his left ear. The rim was now only six feet away. Gasping and grunting, he struggled toward it. He felt a slug chew at the heel of his right boot as the snow-covered ledge came within his grasp. Then his hand slipped and he fell back into the bush he was using to propel himself over the top. "No!" he gasped, his throat on fire. "You're not going to get me!"

Doubling his effort, he coiled and then uncoiled his body, propelling himself up from the shrub and gripping the small trunk of a tree on top. Bullets whistled and hummed over his head while others bounced off the face of the cliff. Suddenly he was over the edge, rolling in the snow, and the guards were out of sight.

Clay lay in the safety of his towering perch, sucking hard for air. The snow was falling harder now, and the air was freezing and burned his lungs, but he did not care. He had eluded capture and death. Now he would find a hiding place and wait out the guards, which the falling snow would help him to accomplish.

From below Clay could hear the guards cursing and talking loudly. Crawling carefully to the rim of the cliff, he peered down. They were mounting their horses, and the one who seemed to be in charge was swearing profusely. "He ain't worth it," the man shouted angrily. "It's snowing harder. By the time we'd get up there, he could be hiding in any one of a thousand places. We'd just freeze our tails off trying to find him. Let's go."

Clay was elated. He watched them ride slowly into the woods and disappear; then, rising to his feet, he checked himself over. No blood. Miraculously, he had escaped being hit. His right coat sleeve had a five-inch rip along the forearm, and the heel was shot off his right boot, but that was the extent of the damage. He breathed a prayer of thanks and blinked away tears of relief. Exhaustion and cold were now crawling into him, and a shudder shot through his body as he headed over the snow-covered ground into more forest. He must not give in to the fatigue, and walking would help stave off the cold.

Clay did not know where he was, but he decided to keep moving until he came upon a stream to follow or found an area inhabited by people. Unaware that he had bypassed the town of Parkdale by getting so far from the main road, he groped his way northwestward, though he had lost all sense of direction.

About an hour had passed when two wagons rumbled along a road off to his right, roughly a hundred feet below where he stood. He saw nothing ahead of them, so he looked back along the trail they had left in the snow. A long, squat building with smoke curling invitingly from its chimney sat just a few hundred yards away.

He hurried in the direction of the building. As he neared it, he saw several saddled horses and a single wagon standing in front. Peering through the swirling snow, he made out a partly obscured sign over the door. It read: Spike Buck Trading Post. A smaller sign just below it advised that the place was also a way station for the Wells Fargo Stagelines Company.

Trading posts sold clothing and footwear, Clay reminded himself. Somehow he had to rid himself of the prison grays and get into civilian clothes—and he had to do it without being seen.

It took him ten minutes to work his way through the

surrounding woods to the rear of the trading post. A number of horses stood in a corral next to a small barn, their heads bent low and their tails turned into the wind. Clay figured them to be Wells Fargo property. Bending low and moving swiftly through the falling snow, he made his way to the back door of the building. He could hear voices inside, although they seemed relatively distant. Cautiously, he lifted the latch and inched the heavy door open. No one was in sight, but to his satisfaction, there were several long tables just inside the rear of the trading post where dry goods of every description were on display. And alongside the clothing were several shelves of boots. Even more fortunate was the fact that the area was out of view of the front of the building.

Dropping to his hands and knees, Clay crawled inside and pulled the door shut. While quickly selecting items that would fit him, he heard a man telling someone that he was there to meet his mother, who was coming in on the stage from Pueblo. The other person—who was apparently the owner of the trading post as well as the Fargo agent—responded in a deep voice, which indicated that he was probably a large man.

Listening to the agent, Clay learned that the stage was on its last run of the season. Its official final stop was Aspen; however, the stage driver and shotgunner lived in Fairplay, and they would drive the vehicle there to wait for spring.

Collecting a pair of boots, a black Stetson, pants, shirt, gloves, and a plaid mackinaw, Clay carefully made his way out the back door and then ran to the barn. There, he hurriedly changed clothes, burying the prison uniform and old boots under a huge pile of hay. Two saddle horses occupied stalls inside the barn, and the escapee bridled and saddled the strongest-looking one and led it out the back side. Opening the corral gate, he led the horse through and then closed the gate and mounted up. Once again having his bearings, he rode through the woods for a quarter mile to avoid being seen, then turned onto the road and headed west.

The wind plucked hard at the black Stetson. Clay tightened the hat on his head and dug his heels into the horse's flanks. Time was of the essence. He had to reach Buckskin Pass while it was still accessible.

Clay had ridden only about three miles and was galloping down a steep hill when the horse suddenly lost its footing in the snow. It went down head over heels, throwing him from the saddle in time to escape being crushed. He landed in a large bush, adding to the scratches on his face, but otherwise he was not hurt, and his new clothes were not torn.

Scrambling to his feet, he hurried over to the horse, which was lying in the snow, whinnying in pain. The animal had broken its left foreleg and did not even attempt to stand. Shaking his head, the tall man brushed the snow off his jacket and murmured, "Well, old boy, I sure wish I had a gun. You're hurting bad, and there's no way you'll ever get better."

Cursing his bad luck, Clay knew it would be too dangerous to go back to the trading post and try to take the other horse. He would just have to walk up the road until he found a ranch where he could steal another one. As much as stealing went against him, leaving the injured horse in misery was bothering him more. But he had no choice. He had no way of killing the horse, and he would freeze to death himself if he stayed there.

Pulling up the collar of the mackinaw and turtling his head deeply into it, he started trudging through the snow, heading west along the road.

Chapter Six

As the stagecoach climbed higher into the mountains, the icy wind knifed across the faces of Claude Overstreet and Bill Mundy and pelted them with snow. The rapidly deepening snow was forcing the six-up team to labor harder, and the steep grades were becoming increasingly more difficult to navigate.

"There's one good thing about this storm," Mundy remarked to his partner above the rattle of harness and the howl of the wind.

Head bent against the driving snow, Overstreet asked, "What's that?"

"It'll probably keep the Utes holed up so's they won't be jumpin' us."

"I'll buy that," the experienced driver agreed. "Of course, we've got a long way to go before we're safe from them redskins. And I sure hope we don't have this kind of weather all the way to Aspen."

Mundy laughed hollowly. "If this keeps up, we won't be gettin' to Aspen till spring. We'll have to wait out the winter at Salida or Buena Vista."

"Let's hope not. I want to warm my feet by my own fire in my own little cabin in Fairplay."

"Sounds good," Mundy said, tugging at his coat collar. "Especially right now!"

Down below, the passengers huddled beneath the buffalo-hide blankets in the dimly lit coach. Every so often one of the youths pulled back a drawn curtain to see where they were, allowing light to briefly penetrate the gloom. But the leather flap was quickly dropped into place to keep out the wind, throwing the travelers back into murkiness.

Even in the indistinct light, however, Barbara LaBonde could read the curiosity in the eyes of the two older women as they continually studied her battered face. Finally Mattie Phelps apparently worked up sufficient courage to match her level of curiosity and said point-blank, "Mrs. LaBonde, I was wondering how you got those bruises on your face."

Though Barbara had remonstrated Gene Fletcher for his prying, she found it hard to be short-tempered with this kind old woman. However, the truth would be embarrassing, so she hedged by replying quietly, "I . . . uh, fell, Mrs. Phelps."

When Martha Bowman raised her eyebrows and flicked a glance at the brunette, Barbara blushed, but she said no more.

The snow was still falling heavily as the stagecoach pulled into the first way station—the Spike Buck Trading Post. Claude Overstreet drew the stage up as close to the door of the trading post as he could and called down, "Okay, folks, here we are. There'll be a warm fire inside, and the privies are around the back. You can get to 'em through the back door of the building."

As the passengers alighted from the coach, Martha Bowman was met by her son. She bid the passengers good-bye and was quickly escorted to a waiting wagon. The remaining passengers visited the privies, and then they all huddled around the stove for the first real warmth they had known for hours. Talking among themselves, they watched through the frost-traced window as the big, husky station agent helped the stage crew hitch a fresh team to the coach.

When the vehicle was ready to travel, driver and shotgunner followed the agent through the door, stomping snow from their boots. They peeled off their coats and took ten minutes to thaw their bodies next to the stove while chewing on some beef jerky and hardtack. Soon it was time to travel again, and as the crewmen put their coats back on, Overstreet said to his passengers, "Next station is at a little town called Ford. As the crow flies, it's only about eleven or twelve miles away . . . but we ain't crows, so we gotta take the road. And it's a windin' one with plenty of ups and downs, and they're all steep. By the time we get to Ford, we'll have actually covered fifteen or sixteen miles. We'll spend the night there, and you'll be glad to know they're equipped with plenty of beds. They'll feed us a good supper tonight and then give us a hearty breakfast in the mornin' to see us on our way."

Making their way outside into the frigid air, the travelers noted that the snowfall was diminishing, which pleased Overstreet considerably. It also eased the minds of his passengers, who settled back under the heavy blankets in their same seats as before, ready for the next leg of the journey. With a jerk, the stagecoach started forward, and it was obvious from the speed they were making that the fresh team of horses was eager to go. Muscles flexing, they plowed vigorously through the snow, clouds of vapor streaming from their flared nostrils.

The coach had traveled about three miles and was heading down a steep grade when it suddenly came to a stop. Gene Fletcher opened the door just as the crew climbed down and asked, "What are you stopping for?"

"There's an injured horse over there," the driver said over his shoulder as he and the shotgun guard trudged through the snow toward the animal. Fletcher followed Overstreet and Mundy to the animal. Then the two youths also alighted.

"Leg's broke," observed Overstreet, making a quick examination of the horse. "From the looks of the snow right here, I'd say it fell and dumped its rider. Why in tarnation would a man leave an animal in a fix like this? Only humane thing to do is shoot it. Seems to me—"

"Mr. Overstreet!" called Leonard Robertson. "I think that's the rider coming now."

Every eye followed the youth's finger as he pointed up the road. A tall man wearing a black Stetson and a plaid mackinaw was running toward them.

"Must be," agreed the driver, nodding.

They waited for the man to arrive, then Overstreet demanded, "This your horse, mister?"

"Yes, sir," the tall, handsome man replied. "We took a spill a few minutes ago. I was just a piece up the road when I heard your stage and hurried back."

"Looks like you got your face scratched up some," observed the driver.

"Oh, ah . . . yeah. I landed in that bush over there. Face first, I guess."

"Was you just gonna leave him here like this?" queried Overstreet. "I mean, least you could do was put a bullet in his head."

"I would have," replied Clay Edwards, "but I'm not carrying a gun. I was hoping to find a ranch up here a ways and borrow one."

"Why didn't you go back to the trading post?" asked Gene Fletcher. "You must have passed it if you were riding this way. They'd have loaned you a gun."

"I'm a stranger in these parts," replied Clay, "but I did come past the trading post. I just thought there might be a ranch somewhat closer."

Noticing that Bill Mundy was studying his face, Clay turned to the shotgunner. A look of recognition came over Mundy's face, and he declared, "I know you! You're Clay Edwards, the gunfighter!"

Claude Overstreet's head whipped around, and Gene Fletcher's mouth fell open.

Nodding, Clay responded, "You're right. Have we met somewhere?"

"Not exactly," replied the shotgunner. "But I once saw you come to a marshal's aid when he was about to be cut down by a passel of miscreants. It was somewhere in central Colorado." Smiling, Mundy added, "You saved that lawman's life, no doubt about it."

Clay nodded silently. Then he gestured toward the Colt .44 on Mundy's hip and asked, "How about letting me borrow your revolver? I'd like to put this poor beast out of its misery."

"Sure," Mundy replied, hero worship evident in his eyes. Pulling the gun from its holster, he handed it to Clay butt first.

Stepping to the downed animal, the ex-gunfighter thumbed back the hammer and fired. The gun roared, its report echoing across the mountains. Handing the Colt back to Mundy, Clay sighed and murmured thanks.

"Don't mention it. By the way, my name's Bill Mundy," the shotgunner said, holstering the gun and extending his hand. While they shook hands, Mundy remarked, "I got to admit I'm a bit puzzled, Mr. Edwards. I can't feature you goin' anywhere without your gun."

"That's because I'm not a gunfighter anymore."

Clearly astonished, Mundy gasped, "You're not?"

"Nope. Hung my gun up two years ago to take up ranching. I, uh . . . work for Bart Jarrell at the Diamond J Ranch over near Gunnison."

"You're kinda far from home, ain'tcha?" the driver asked.

"Well, I'm headed north to Buckskin Pass to see a man on some very important business."

"I see," Overstreet mused. "Well, this here stage is bound for Aspen, and we've got a seat available if you want it."

Thinking fast, Clay said, "I appreciate that, Mr. Overstreet, but . . . well, truth is, I'm what you'd call financially embarrassed. My wallet got stolen from my hotel room in Canon City, and I haven't got a cent on me. I was hoping to find a rancher who'd let me have a horse on my word until I could get home and send him the money. I . . . I was going to see if he'd lend me some eating money, too."

Bill Mundy's eyes were still lit with admiration. "I don't have enough money to lend you to buy a horse, Mr. Edwards, but I think I can part with enough to buy meals for you for a week or so. Wouldn't be a loan, though. I'll just make it a gift."

"I can't let you do that, Mr. Mundy," said Clay. "I'd rather it was just a loan."

"We'll argue about that later," said Mundy, pulling his wallet and handing over ten dollars. "And please call me Bill."

The grateful Edwards smiled. "Thanks, Bill. Much obliged. And please call me Clay."

"Tell you what," said Overstreet. "Let's take your saddle and bridle off the horse. We'll toss 'em up in the rack. You can ride with us until you decide to make a deal on a horse. If you should ride all the way to Aspen, I'll take an IOU, and you can send the money to the Aspen office when you get home. How's that?"

"I'm much obliged to you, Mr. Overstreet," Clay declared. He then removed the tack from the dead horse and hefted it back to the stagecoach.

As he turned to climb into the coach, Gene Fletcher extended his hand and introduced himself. "I've heard of you, too, Edwards. Pleasure to meet you in person."

Clay asked, "How far are you traveling?"

"All the way to Aspen—or actually, I'll ride on over to Fairplay with the crew. I own a saloon there, and I was looking into opening up a new one in Pueblo. You ought to get into the saloon business, Edwards. Better money than ranching, by far."

"No thanks," Clay responded. "I like the smell of horses, hay, and barns better than the smell of whiskey, cigarette smoke, and cheap perfume."

Fletcher shrugged. "Every man to his own poison," he said with a wry grin.

Clay took the seat between Gene Fletcher and Mattie Phelps, and the remaining passengers introduced themselves. The ex-gunfighter was immensely relieved that none of the travelers was aware that he had been in prison—or that he had escaped.

Mattie Phelps remarked, "I take it from the way the menfolk have reacted that you're famous for what you do, Mr. Edwards." Glancing at Barbara, she continued, "But we ladies don't follow gunfighting and that kind of thing, so we don't know you, do we Mrs. LaBonde?"

Barbara's face colored slightly. "Actually, I do, Mrs. Phelps," she said somewhat timidly. "That is, I know of Mr. Edwards's reputation."

Smiling, Clay asked, "Should I be flattered or sorry, Mrs. LaBonde?"

"Neither," Barbara responded, unsmiling and without elaboration.

Gene Fletcher elbowed Clay and smirked, but he ignored him and settled back in the seat. He had long been a student of people, and traveling in such close quarters gave him the opportunity to flex his observations. Mattie Phelps was a typical woman of her age, and her attitude toward his past as a gunfighter was exactly what he would have expected. Jim McLaughlin and Leonard Robertson seemed to be fine, sincere young men, and though Clay regretted that they wore guns at such a young age, they seemed to have clear-thinking heads on their shoulders and he was pleased when they explained that they were heading to Aspen to get into ranching.

Gene Fletcher was another story. Clay did not trust the man. There was something in his ice-blue eyes that caused a certain uneasiness. He would bear watching.

Clay gazed casually at Barbara LaBonde. Despite her bruises, he found her strikingly beautiful, and the lustrous dark hair that spilled from under her hat to her shoulders added to her beauty. Her features were delicate yet sensuous, but her eyes displayed a profound sadness. He assumed the sadness had a connection with the obvious beating she had received, and he wondered if it had been at the hands of a brutal husband.

Apparently noticing Clay studying Barbara, Mattie

broke the silence of the coach by saying, "Mrs. LaBonde told us she fell, Mr. Edwards. Poor little thing. I think she must have fallen against some brute of a man's fists."

Clay looked back at Barbara. For a moment the interior of the coach was utterly silent. Then Barbara LaBonde's face crumpled and she whimpered slightly as tears rushed to her eyes. Burying her face in her hands, she bent over, sobbing.

"Oh dear," gasped Mattie, looking around at the men. "I've gone and said too much."

Clay Edwards leaned across and laid a tender hand on Barbara's shoulder, asking softly, "Is there anything I can do to help, ma'am?"

With her face still pressed into her hands, the brunette wordlessly shook her head. After a few moments she seemed to have brought her emotions under control, and she sat up, her mouth quivering. Reaching beneath the heavy blanket, she produced a handkerchief from the pocket of her coat, dabbing at her eyes and then blowing her nose. She swallowed hard and murmured, "Thank you, Mr. Edwards, but there's nothing anyone can do."

Mattie quickly apologized, saying, "I'm terribly sorry, my dear. I didn't mean to upset you so."

"It's all right, Mrs. Phelps," Barbara said kindly. "You were only showing concern. I lied to you. Please forgive me for that. As you have already figured out, I didn't fall. My husband beat me up. It wasn't the first time, and I feared it would not be the last." She paused for a moment, then added softly, "That's why I left him and am going to live with my sister."

"Oh, you poor dear," Mattie said sympathetically.

The old woman's concern acted as a release for the emotions that had been dammed up inside the beautiful woman, for Barbara poured out her story in a torrent of words. When she had finished telling of Jack LaBonde's drinking, womanizing, and physical brutalities since the first week of their marriage, Clay Edwards remarked in a voice filled with anger, "No one can blame you for leaving a man like that, ma'am. If you'll pardon my saying so, a husband who'll manhandle his wife is lower than a snake's belly. He ought to be horsewhipped."

Barbara glanced at Clay but did not respond.

The snow had stopped falling and the clouds were breaking up overhead when the stagecoach swung off the road at Ford, Colorado, and hauled up in front of the way station. As the passengers got off the coach, darkness was fast descending and the temperature was dropping rapidly.

Passengers and crew entered the station building and were welcomed by the agent and his wife. The travelers were assigned rooms and beds, and then they warmed themselves by a large fireplace while supper was set out on a long table. Clay Edwards sat across from Barbara LaBonde, which obviously irritated Gene Fletcher, who crowded as close to her as he could.

While they ate, Clay tried to encourage the beautiful young woman, attempting to ease the pain she was clearly feeling; however, Barbara did not respond well. Though she was not unkind or rude, she was quite cool and aloof.

Only half listening to the ex-gunfighter, Barbara nonetheless found herself admiring his striking good looks and muscular physique—though she wondered whether his display of concern and kindess was but a façade. Did he perhaps have a wife somewhere that he had mistreated? After all, she told herself, those women Jack hung out with certainly didn't see him for what he actually was. If they really knew the beast that lurked beneath the charming image, they wouldn't go near him. Perhaps Clay Edwards was also a beast in disguise. Certainly that's what her father and brothers were—and all men were the same.

At daylight the next morning Claude Overstreet and Bill Mundy left the warmth of the station building for the barn to harness up a fresh team and then hitch them to the stagecoach. The frosty air bit at them unmercifully, and snow blanketed everything, although the sky was cloudless and the eastern horizon, ragged with mountain peaks, was coming alive with a brilliant sunrise.

Twenty minutes later Overstreet drove the coach from the barn to the front of the station building while Mundy walked alongside. The snow crunched loudly under their boots as the driver and shotgunner entered the station to the smell of hot coffee mingled with the aroma of scrambled eggs, home-fried potatoes, sausage, and pancakes. "Sure am glad the storm's over," said Overstreet.

"Me, too," said Mundy, taking off his coat. "I don't want any more snow till we park the coach in your barn at Fairplay."

Clay Edwards sat across from Barbara again. As they began to eat, he smiled and said, "Good morning, ma'am."

"Good morning," the brunette replied coolly.

"Did you sleep well?" he asked.

"Yes, thank you. And you?" she asked politely.

"Like an innocent baby," he responded. Then, chuckling, he added, "Only I didn't wet the bed."

The unexpected quip clearly took Barbara by surprise, and she laughed heartily.

"It's good to know you can actually do that," he commented quietly.

"Do what?"

"Laugh."

"Oh. Well, Mr. Edwards, I haven't had much to laugh about lately."

"I understand, ma'am," he said softly. He sipped his coffee and then remarked, "I think the bruises have lightened some."

"I hope so," she replied. "I look so awful."

"If I may say so, ma'am, I don't think there's any way you could look awful. You are a very beautiful young woman."

Barbara was obviously thrown off balance by his words, and she crimsoned slightly and quickly took a bite of pancake.

Feeling hostile eyes on him, Clay glanced over and saw Gene Fletcher staring at him, but the man remained silent.

Claude Overstreet joined the others at the table and announced, "We'll be pullin' out at six-thirty sharp, and our next stop ain't till Salida, twenty-four miles from here. Coverin' that kind of distance in this country after a snowstorm will take us every bit of all day, so we'll have to take it real easy on the horses. But don't worry. We're carryin' plenty of food and water." Shaking his head, he went on, "But tomorrow will be tougher yet, 'cause we'll have to cover twenty-seven miles between Salida and Buena Vista."

When they were ready to travel, Overstreet and Mundy escorted the passengers out to the coach, and the bitterly cold air went right through them.

"Whooee, it's cold!" Jim McLaughlin yelped.

Overstreet laughed and looked back at the handsome youth, declaring, "This mountain air bites you so hard it leaves toothmarks on your cheeks!"

Everyone boarded the stagecoach, and the vehicle started its run, plodding along slowly on the snow-covered road. Driver and shotgunner squinted against the sun's harsh glare off the gleaming mantle of white that surrounded them, and the savage wind clawed at their heavy coats and plucked at their broad-brimmed hats.

They had been traveling for just over two hours when Mundy heard a horse snort from behind the coach, and being alert for any sign of Utes, he swiveled around on the seat, bringing up his shotgun. Seeing his partner's reaction, Overstreet turned to look as well. Both were surprised to see a lone rider drawing close, leading a saddled, riderless horse. The man quickly pulled alongside the coach and shouted, "Hey, driver! Stop the coach!"

Inside the vehicle, Barbara LaBonde's head snapped up, and she immediately pulled back the leather curtain from her window and looked out. Her face paled, and she breathed an oath.

"What is it, Mrs. LaBonde?" Clay asked, seeing the mixture of fear and anger on her face.

"It's my husband," Barbara said through clenched teeth.

Jack LaBonde leapt from his horse as Overstreet hauled the coach to a stop. "What do you want?" the driver asked.

"You've got my wife aboard," replied Jack, reaching for the door handle. Jerking open the coach door, Jack's eyes found Barbara's and he ordered, "Come on! You're goin' home with me!"

Barbara could tell that Jack had been drinking, but he was not drunk. Her voice was as cold as the gusting wind as she countered, "Go away, Jack! Leave me alone!"

Insistent, Jack shouted, "Either you get out of there yourself or I'll pull you out! You're goin' home with me!"

Furious and humiliated, the brunette retorted, "I have no home, Jack—and I'm not going anywhere with you! Go away and let me be!"

Knowing that he was looking at the brute who had beaten the lovely young woman, anger surged through Clay Edwards. He leaned past her and said heatedly, "The lady just told you to leave her alone, mister! I suggest you climb on your horse and vamoose!"

Fury twisted Jack's mottled face. "You mind your own business!"

"I'm making it my business, LaBonde!" Clay shouted back. "Any man who would beat up a woman as you've done to your wife is nothing but scum!"

Hissing through his teeth for Clay to butt out, Jack grabbed Barbara's coat and yanked her through the door, throwing her in the snow. He screamed at her like a madman, commanding, "Get up and climb in the saddle, Barbara! Right now!"

The brunette struggled to her feet, but instead of complying, she grabbed for the revolver on her husband's hip. Jack sidestepped her and slapped her across the face, and Barbara fell backward in the snow.

Enraged, Clay leapt through the open doorway and tackled the stocky LaBonde, and the two men rolled in the snow, legs and arms flailing. Jack swore at Clay, swinging both fists but missing. Clay punched back, stunning his opponent momentarily, and he stood and turned toward Barbara. She was getting to her feet, shaking her head to clear it. "Jim! Leonard!" Clay called. "Help Mrs. LaBonde into the coach!"

As the young men scrambled out of the coach and went to assist the brunette, Jack LaBonde rolled to his knees while Clay was facing the coach and grabbed his feet. With a jerk he felled the ex-gunfighter, then kicked him in the face. The maddened husband then leapt to his feet and whipped out his gun, cocking the hammer. Lining the gun on his estranged wife, he bellowed, "I'll kill you!"

Reacting instantly, Clay rose and lunged at Jack, grasping the man's gun hand and forcing the muzzle away from Barbara just as the gun roared. The bullet missed her by inches, plowing into the rear boot as Mattie Phelps screamed with fright. Clay then wrenched his foe's wrist and forced the gun from his hand, while the two youths took hold of Barbara's arms and helped her back into the stagecoach.

The men traded several blows, and then Clay got in a solid punch, flattening his adversary in the snow an arm's length from the revolver. Seeing the weapon, Jack reached for the gun and cocked it, ready to shoot. But Clay was too fast for him, and he dived for Jack's gun hand and turned the muzzle away. Grunting and swearing as they rose to their feet, they struggled for supremacy. Jack's finger was on the trigger as he tried to force the muzzle against Clay.

Suddenly the revolver went off with a deafening roar. Jack stiffened, a shocked look on his face, and then crumpled to the ground with a slug in his heart. As the echo of the shot slowly died away, Jack LaBonde also died.

Kneeling beside the sprawled form, Clay felt the sides of the man's neck. Then he rose slowly and turned toward the coach, addressing Barbara, who was watching out the window. "Mrs. LaBonde, your husband's dead."

Barbara showed no emotion. She only nodded, then sat back in the seat.

Jack LaBonde was buried in the snow next to a huge boulder without his widow shedding a tear. When Clay

Edwards climbed into the coach wearing Jack's gun belt around his waist, Jim McLaughlin remarked, "I thought you weren't going to wear a gun anymore, Mr. Edwards."

Clay shook his head and said, "I wasn't, but Claude and Bill told me last night that there's a chance we could encounter some hostiles at any time. I think they had Utes in mind, but it seems like a good idea to be ready for anything—or anyone."

After the two saddle horses were tied behind the coach, it pulled out and rolled up the grade with the draft horses straining against the harness. Suddenly Barbara LaBonde took out her handkerchief and began to weep.

Clay leaned toward her and murmured, "I'm sorry about having to kill your husband, ma'am. I didn't have any choice."

The brunette shook her head. "You don't have to apologize, Mr. Edwards. I'm not crying over Jack. These are tears of relief. He killed whatever love I had for him the first week of our marriage, and he dealt me nothing but heartache and misery ever since. I guess I sound cruel and heartless, but I'm glad that he's gone. The Lord knows I never wished him dead, but now that it's done, I do not wish him back."

Clay settled back in his seat and said, "You don't sound cruel and heartless at all, ma'am. If you'll excuse my saying so, the only thing you did wrong was being too forgiving for too long and not leaving him sooner."

Barbara smiled weakly and said, "You're right, Mr. Edwards, and aside from that, I owe you my life. If you hadn't stopped him, Jack would have shot me. Thank you."

"Glad I could be of service to you, ma'am," the handsome cowboy said softly. "And I'd do it again if the occasion called for it." He smiled. "Let's hope that doesn't happen."

Chapter Seven

The six-horse team continued to plod through the deep snow, straining hard into the harness at times to keep the stagecoach moving. Four hours had passed since the travelers had left Jack LaBonde's body behind, buried deep in the snow, when Claude Overstreet pulled rein at the crest of a long, steep incline. The horses were breathing hard; it was obvious that they needed a rest.

Overstreet climbed down from the box with Bill Mundy following. The driver opened the door and told the passengers, "Gotta rest the horses, folks. The wind's a bit nasty out here, but maybe you'd like to get out and stretch your legs or use the woods, if you have to. Might be a good time to eat some chow, too."

Agreeing with the suggestions, the travelers stepped out of the coach. Despite the merciless wind, it felt good to them to unfold their cramped limbs. While walking about, they ate beef jerky and hardtack, stomping their feet and working their arms intermittently to keep the circulation going. Fewer than ten minutes of the icy blasts was enough to drive the passengers back into the relative warmth of the coach.

Several minutes after that, as the driver and shotgunner climbed back to the box and covered their legs with buffalo hide, they assessed the sky. Heavy, dark clouds were gathering in the west, warning of another impending storm.

Cursing, Overstreet snapped the reins, and the coach lurched forward.

It took almost a half hour for the stagecoach to reach the bottom of the long, steep slope that ended in a huge, bowl-shaped valley half covered with expanses of pine forest. Encircling the valley were jagged peaks blanketed by snow. The barely visible road ran along the edge of a broad, snow-covered lake. Shortly after the coach had descended into the valley, one of the horses began to limp. Overstreet halted the vehicle beside the frozen lake and slid to the ground. The driver paused at the covered window long enough to explain the stop to the passengers and then moved to the team. The second horse on the left-hand side was bobbing its head and raising its front foreleg.

Cursing the savage wind, Overstreet slipped in between the animals to take a look at the hoof. Mundy, a heavy scarf covering all of his face except his eyes, watched his colleague carefully and waited for the verdict. Presently the driver let go of the horse's hoof and shouted up to his shotgunner, "Shoe's comin' loose. We'll have to nail it back on, but it'll mean takin' the horse out of the harness to do it. No room to work in there."

While Overstreet and Mundy endured the cold and unhitched the team to separate the animal, the four men alighted from the coach to stretch again. Barbara LaBonde and Mattie Phelps chose to stay inside, huddled in the buffalo-hide blankets, and Clay Edwards and Gene Fletcher stood just outside the door, talking to the women.

Jim McLaughlin and Leonard Robertson walked around, talking excitedly about their new venture. While they talked, they peered at the surrounding mountain peaks, which were rapidly being covered by ominous, wind-driven clouds.

Jim commented, "If we get much more snow, Len, old pal, we're not going to see our new home until mid-April."

Shrugging, the slightly younger youth said, "Mr.

Overstreet is wanting to get home pretty bad. I think it'll take a whole lot of snow to make him give up."

Jim chuckled and wiped his runny nose. "Yeah, I guess you're right about—" He abruptly stopped speaking, and his face paled.

Glancing at his friend, Leonard saw the look of terror on Jim's face and asked, "What is it?"

"Look up there, Len!"

The seventeen-year-old suddenly felt frightened. "Where? I don't see anything."

Raising a gloved hand, Jim pointed and said, "Right up there on that ledge, between those two patches of pines. See them?"

Leonard Robertson's mouth dropped open as he discerned four dark, fur-clad men. The sight served to ice up his body more than the wintry wind had. "Indians!" he gasped.

Abruptly the Indians turned and dashed into the trees, vanishing from sight.

"Come on!" Jim yelped. "We gotta tell the others!"

The youths ran toward the coach, shouting, "Indians! We saw Indians!"

Clay's head whipped around and Fletcher stiffened, while Barbara and Mattie looked terror-stricken. The crewmen left their chore and joined the others, and Overstreet demanded, "Are you sure?"

"Absolutely!" answered Len, pointing toward the ledge where the Indians had been. "There were four of 'em! Right up there!"

"When they saw us looking at them, they ran into the trees," Jim added.

Clay Edwards, his eyes fixed on the spot, said evenly, "If you saw Utes, it's because they wanted you to see them. They're using scare tactics."

"Well, it worked!" choked out young Robertson. "I'm scared!"

Mundy shook his head. "Bein' out here in the open sure ain't gonna help us"—he gestured at the now heavily falling snow—"any more than this stuff will! Let's get the horses hitched up and move! Fast!"

Nodding, Overstreet responded, "If we're lucky, this snow'll work in our favor. Maybe them redskins'll go hole up somewhere, 'stead of hittin' us."

While Clay helped the crew get the horses back in place, the other passengers boarded the coach. Then the driver issued Clay and Fletcher Winchester seven-shot rifles. "I hope we don't have to use these," Overstreet declared, "but we better be prepared, just in case." Looking at the youths, he said, "You boys know how to use them revolvers of yours?"

"Yes, sir!" they answered in unison.

Overstreet nodded. He gave the passengers a few quick instructions on what to do in case they were attacked, and then he made his way to the top of the box. As the stage headed out, the crewmen peered through the windblown curtain of snow, watching intently for Indians.

Inside the coach Barbara sat across from Mattie, holding her hands. The elderly woman was quaking and sobbing hysterically. Suddenly she shrieked, "They're going to scalp us! They're going to scalp us!"

Shaking her head, the brunette responded softly, "You heard what Mr. Overstreet said: There's a possibility the Indians won't attack us while it's snowing. And it's certainly snowing harder by the minute." She smiled encouragingly. "No doubt they want to stay warm and dry, too. Chances are they were just going back to their camp when they saw us."

She glanced at Clay, who was seated beside her, but instead of responding, he began rolling up the curtains, letting in the biting wind and snow. When the other passengers protested, he explained, "We have to be able to see out. I know it'll be cold and wet, but we don't have a choice. In case the Utes come at us, we must be alert and ready to start shooting."

The ex-gunfighter felt the fear of the other passengers, and while he knew they had to keep their eyes peeled for the hostiles, if their minds could be diverted, it might help calm them—or at least keep them from panicking.

Pulling the collar of his mackinaw up tight around his neck, Clay looked at the two youths and said, "You fellas mentioned that you were starting up a ranch together. That seems mighty enterprising of you. I'd be interested in knowing a bit more about how you're going to accomplish it."

Jim McLaughlin remarked, "Well, my pa died not long ago and left the family ranch to my older brother. But he left a decent amount of money to me, so I talked Len into working on a new spread with me up north." He then chuckled, adding, "But you're a lot more interesting than either of us, Mr. Edwards. I'd appreciate knowing more about your career. You know, how you became a gunfighter, the number of men you killed, and why you decided to give it up to do ranching."

It was evident that the others were equally curious, but Clay merely replied, "I really don't think my life as a gunfighter is all that interesting."

"If you don't mind telling us," cut in Len, not taking his eyes from the window, "I'd sure like to hear about it."

Clay rubbed the back of his neck and sighed. "I don't really like talking about myself—and especially not about a part of my life I consider over and done with, but . . ." After a brief pause, he began, "I became a gunfighter without intending to. Like you fellas, I was raised on a ranch. . . . One day, when I was eighteen, I had gone into town. There, three young toughs decided to beat me up, for no reason whatever. Well, to make my story short, while defending myself I banged the head of one of them against the hitch rail, and he went out cold. The town marshal finally came to my rescue and broke up the fight, and the fella who was unconscious was taken to the doctor. It turned out the guy had a cracked skull and died the next day."

"Oh, how awful!" exclaimed Barbara, who was listening intently.

Nodding, Clay said, "That it was . . . and worse for me, his older brother was a gunfighter, name of Emory Connor. The dead guy's pals informed me that Connor'd surely come gunning for me, so I'd better be ready. I decided they were right, and I learned how to quick-draw. I found I had a natural knack for it. It took Connor about three months to show up, and by that time I was pretty fast. We squared off and—well, since I'm alive and telling this story, you know how it turned out."

"So what happened after that?" queried Jim, his eyes shining with interest as he watched Clay.

"Word spread that I had taken out Connor, and I started being challenged."

"It seems to me there can be only one end to a career like that," Barbara mused. "A man who lives by the gun is eventually going to meet up with a man faster than he is. He has to end up dying with a bullet in him."

Clay regarded her intently for a moment, then said, "Unless he quits before that inevitable man crosses his path."

"But how does a gunfighter quit, Mr. Edwards? I realize you took off your gun and went back to ranching, but won't somebody come along and force you to put on a gun and face him?"

"He can try," replied Clay, "but if I outright refuse to put on a gun, I'm safe. No challenger would want to gun me down if I'm not wearing a weapon. He'd be marked as a coward for killing an unarmed man, and his career'd be over."

Barbara eyed her husband's gun adorning Clay's hip. "But you put on Jack's gun. What will happen now?"

He shook his head. "This is just for use if we have to battle the Utes. Once we're out of danger, off comes the gun."

"I hope it works for you," Barbara said with a weak smile.

He smiled back. "It has for two years."

"So you returned to ranching when you hung up your gun because that's what you'd done before—is that it, Mr. Edwards?" Jim queried.

"That's it," the ex-gunfighter replied.

"You didn't tell us how many men you've killed in gunfights," the youth pressed.

"I don't really know for sure," Clay answered, side-stepping the question.

"But didn't you notch your gun?" asked Len, looking briefly at Clay.

Sniffing derisively, Clay replied, "Only blowhards do that—and most of them don't live long enough to get more than one or two notches carved."

"Oh," Len responded, clearly disappointed to learn the truth of the subject. Persisting, he added, "But you must have some idea how many."

Clay Edwards turned to look at him and murmured, "I'd rather not discuss it, kid."

Mumbling an apology, Len shifted his concentration out the window.

The other youth asked, "Is the business you have with the man at Buckskin Pass a throwback to your gunfighting days?"

C. K. Moxley's face flashed through Clay's mind, and he felt his anger rising. Without answering, he turned and looked out the window, and everyone else fell silent as well. Staring into the falling snow, he saw that the stagecoach had topped the steep incline and now started winding around the side of a mountain. Through the swirling flakes Clay could see a sheer drop several yards from the road.

Gene Fletcher finally broke the silence by saying, "Mrs. LaBonde, how about if I call you Barbara? I mean, seeing as how we're riding this stage together, and especially with the danger we're sharing, I figure we might consider ourselves friends."

"I am not your enemy, Mr. Fletcher," Barbara responded coolly, "but I hardly consider us to be friends. When this ride is over, we will never see each other again, and therefore please continue to address me formally."

Shifting in the seat, Fletcher cleared his throat and said, "You are a widow now, Barbara—a very beautiful one, I might add. Is there anything wrong in my showing interest in a beautiful, unattached woman?"

"There is nothing wrong if the woman is desirous of the interest and responds to it, Mr. Fletcher," she said stiffly. "I am not."

Clay Edwards turned his head, focusing his attention on his fellow passenger. He already had reservations about Fletcher, and the man's insolence in ignoring the brunette's wishes annoyed and angered him.

"I think if you got to know me better, Barbara," insisted the husky saloon owner, "you'd find me quite attractive. Why not give it a chance?"

Barbara's eyes flashed. "I am not interested in giving it a chance, sir," she snapped, "I am not attracted to you in the least—and I am *not* Barbara! To you, if you must address me, I am Mrs. LaBonde!"

Fletcher's ire was evident by the distended veins in his temples. Scowling, his face darkened as he spat, "What's the matter, aren't I good enough for you? Who do you think you are, the Queen of England? Well, let me tell you something! You're nothing but—"

"That's enough, Fletcher!" Clay roared, fixing the man with a withering glare. "Leave the lady alone!"

Fletcher bristled, squaring his shoulders, and lashed back, "You have no claim on her, Edwards, so shut your mouth!"

Clay was blinded with fury. He reached across the coach and grabbed the man by the coat collar, pulling him so close their noses were almost touching. "You'd better shut your own mouth, Fletcher!" he warned. "I'm as sick of listening to you as Mrs. LaBonde is! Only there's one difference—she won't shut your mouth for you, but I will!"

Enraged, Fletcher gave Clay a vicious jab to the chin. Mattie screamed, and the coach came to an abrupt halt as Claude Overstreet shouted from the box, "What's goin' on down there?"

The other passengers attemped to stay out of the way as the two men scuffled. Suddenly Fletcher reached inside his coat and pulled a nickel-plated .32 revolver from a shoulder holster, but Clay reacted quickly and seized the gun, twisting it from his opponent's hand. It clattered to the floor as Clay jerked down on the door handle, flung the door open, and shoved the man out into the snow.

While Bill Mundy scrambled down from his seat to see what was happening, Gene Fletcher rose to his feet from where he had rolled, cursing Clay Edwards, whose muscular body filled the door of the coach. "You aren't getting back in here unless the lady gets an apology!" Clay declared.

Fletcher plodded toward the coach, shouting, "You have no right to keep me out of there!"

Bounding from the vehicle, Clay stood before him, blocking the way, and countered, "We're not discussing rights! We're discussing an apology to Mrs. LaBonde!"

"Nobody gets an apology from me!" the stout-bodied man growled, swinging a fist at Clay's face.

Clay agilely ducked the blow and unleashed a vicious punch of his own, flattening the man in the snow. Fletcher was out cold and was quickly being covered with a blanket of white as Mundy stepped beside Clay and asked what had happened.

After hearing an explanation, the shotgunner agreed that Fletcher had received what was coming to him. Looking down at the unconscious man, Mundy remarked, "He might freeze to death there, Mr. Edwards. Could he make his apology inside the coach after he wakes up?"

"If you insist," Clay replied. Then, picking up the

torpid form, he roughly placed Fletcher back in the coach where he had been sitting.

The ex-gunfighter had just reseated himself when Claude Overstreet hopped down and looked in through the door window. "Might as well tell you now, folks," the driver began, "we're not makin' very good time through this snow. At the rate we're movin', it'll take at least another full day to reach Salida, and with the snow still comin' down hard, it's too dangerous to travel at night. We might get off the road and go over a precipice." He gestured over his shoulder, then continued, "On past trips I've seen a ranch that sits in the valley as we come down off this mountain. We oughtta get down there just about dark, so let's hope the rancher will put us up for the night."

"Do you think we're out of danger from the Indians, Mr. Overstreet?" asked Mattie Phelps in a small voice.

"Can't say for sure, ma'am," replied the weathered driver, "but the storm has kept 'em from attackin' so far, so let's hope they just go away and forget us!"

As the coach moved slowly down the mountain, Gene Fletcher came to. With a sullen look on his face, he glared malevolently at Clay, who said crisply, "Mrs. LaBonde is waiting for her apology."

"Where's my pistol?" Fletcher demanded.

"In my coat pocket," Clay rejoined. "And I said Mrs. LaBonde is waiting for her apology. If she doesn't get it immediately, you'll be walking within ten seconds."

It was evident that Clay meant what he was saying. Grimacing, Fletcher looked at Barbara and said, "I apologize."

"I apologize, Mrs. LaBonde," Clay corrected.

"I apologize, Mrs. LaBonde," the burly man echoed.

Though her demeanor was still aloof, Barbara turned to Clay and said, "Thank you for putting him in his place, Mr. Edwards."

Fletcher scowled at the beautiful widow and the handsome man seated beside her, but he held his tongue, and the journey continued on in silence.

Darkness was blanketing the high mountain country as the coach reached the valley and left the road in the driving storm, heading for the ranch. Light was visible in the windows of the house, and smoke was rising from the chimney. But when the coach rolled to a stop in front of the house and Bill Mundy hopped down and knocked on the door, there was no response. Mundy waited for several seconds and knocked again, louder. Still no one came to the door.

Claude Overstreet then climbed down and told his partner they should check the barn and the sheds. When the crewmen returned, Overstreet told the passengers, "Nobody's out there. If the door's unlocked, we'll just go inside and wait for the owners to return. They can't be far, what with lamps burnin' and a fire goin'."

The shotgunner was about to step onto the porch when the driver called, "Hold it, Bill! Somebody's comin' along the road!"

Two riders were vaguely visible through the falling snow and the near darkness. Mundy stepped off the porch and waited next to the coach and his friend. As the riders drew up, light from the windows revealed them to be women. They were clad in bulky overcoats, and their heads were wrapped in heavy woolen scarves that covered everything but their eyes.

Overstreet touched his hat brim and addressed the older of the two. "Evenin', ma'am. Are you the lady of the house?"

"Yes, I am," responded the woman as she dismounted and ran her gaze over the coach. She stepped close to the driver, pulled the scarf from her mouth, and said, "My name is Jean Hayes." She then gestured toward the younger woman, who was in the process of dismounting. And this is my daughter, Rhonda."

Overstreet quickly explained the plight of the travelers and asked if they could be put up for the night.

The woman responded favorably, asking everyone to come into the house. When they were inside, taking off their coats, gloves, and hats, introductions were made all around. Barbara LaBonde abruptly asked, "You seem upset. Is something wrong?"

Jean Hayes, who appeared to be in her mid-forties, explained that she and her daughter had been out searching for her husband. Alan Hayes had left the house earlier that day to ride to a neighboring ranch, saying he would be back by midafternoon. When he had not returned by then, the two women headed for their neighbor's place, but the storm had forced them to turn back.

Barbara tried to reassure the women, saying that the rancher probably had stayed at the neighbor's house because of the storm. Jean allowed that she had thought the same thing, but fear still showed in her eyes. "I'm pleased to have your company and to give you refuge," she remarked. "And don't worry. There are plenty of beds in the house."

While Clay and the crew went to put the horses and the stagecoach in the barn, Barbara and Mattie began helping the ranch women prepare supper. The brunette volunteered to set the table in the dining room, which was just off the kitchen, and Fletcher, who had stayed in the house, saying he needed to thaw out his half-frozen fingers, took advantage of the opportunity.

Leaving the fireplace, he stepped beside Barbara as she was putting plates on the table. "Really, honey, you and I have to get better acquainted," he breathed. He then put his hand on her shoulder and ran it down her arm to her hand, but she turned and slapped his face.

Clay was just coming through the door from outside, and he stormed across the room. His eyes boring into the husky man, he demanded, "What did you do now?"

"Nothing that concerns you!" Fletcher retorted, rubbing his stinging cheek.

Turning to the brunette, he repeated the question,

and she told him what Fletcher had done. Furious, Clay sank his fingers into the saloon owner's shirt and dragged him toward the door. Fletcher cursed his adversary, trying to free himself, but to no avail. Just then the door opened, and Bill Mundy entered, Claude Overstreet on his heels. Both men jumped out of Clay's way, and the ex-gunfighter pulled his captive out in the snow.

Closing the door and shaking his head, the driver began unbuttoning his coat, remarking, "Mr. Edwards looked a little perturbed. All I can say, ladies, is that what's about to happen out there, you don't want to see."

Sounds of a fierce scuffle came from outside as the women went on preparing supper. Five minutes later a slumping Gene Fletcher was half carried into the house by his opponent. After once again apologizing to Barbara LaBonde, he went to clean his bloody face with water and a towel at the washbasin. While doing so, Fletcher vowed to himself to get even with Clay Edwards.

By nine o'clock everyone had retired for the night, with the angry wind slapping snow against the house. The travelers and their hosts alike all prayed that good news— and good weather—would greet them in the morning.

Chapter Eight

Morning came with a slight wind and a clear sky, and the sun reflecting off the fourteen inches of new snow made it blindingly bright. Jean Hayes had slept little during the night, and she rose from her bed, dressed quickly, and then tiptoed down the long hallway to the kitchen. She would let her daughter and the weary travelers sleep until the house was warm and breakfast was cooking.

After building a fire in the fireplace, she went into the kitchen. Seeing that the firewood box beside the cookstove was nearly empty, she headed for the back porch where dry wood was stacked.

Jean was about to throw on her overcoat before stepping outside when she heard a horse whinny. Her heart began beating harder, and disregarding the icy cold, she flung open the door, exclaiming, "Alan!" There stood her husband's big white stallion, bobbing its head and blowing vapor from its nostrils. Then she noticed that the white coat of the riderless horse was smeared with blood, as was the saddle, and a tingling sensation began at the top of her spine and traveled downward.

Gasping, Jean dashed to the horse to see if the blood was frozen. It was still moist. She drew a shuddering breath and whirled toward the house, almost running headlong into Clay Edwards, who was standing at the door, rubbing sleep from his eyes. "Is that your husband's horse, ma'am?" he asked.

"Yes," Jean half choked, "but there's blood on him, which means Alan's been hurt! But he can't be far away, Mr. Edwards, because the blood's not frozen yet." Darting past the tall man into the house, she said frantically, "I've got to go find him!"

Clay followed her, suggesting, "I'll go, Mrs. Hayes."

Just coming into the kitchen were Gene Fletcher, his face puffy from the beating he had taken, Claude Overstreet, and Bill Mundy. The two youths were coming down the hall. Clay explained to the others what had happened, and then he stepped close to Jean, who was thrusting her arms into her heavy overcoat. "Please, Mrs. Hayes," the ex-gunfighter said, "let me go look for your husband. It might be best that you stay here with your daughter."

"Bill and I will go with you, Clay," spoke up the driver. "The more of us that go, the quicker we'll find him."

"We'll go too," Jim McLaughlin put in, speaking for himself and his friend.

Jean paused with her coat half on. "I hate to trouble you men this way," she murmured.

"You aren't troubling us, ma'am," Clay replied. "We're expressing our gratitude for feeding and sheltering us. Consider it a small repayment. We have two saddle horses with us, but do you have others that the rest of us can use?"

"Certainly."

"Good, then we'll be on our way immediately."

"Don't look at me," said Gene Fletcher. "I'm not going."

"You *are* going," Clay stiffly commanded. "I can't trust you with the women."

Fletcher started to protest, but the look in Clay's eyes declared there would be another beating if he did not acquiesce.

While the men were putting on their coats, Rhonda Hayes entered the room. She glanced from face to face, then looked intently at her mother. Before the young woman could ask what was going on, Jean explained, "Father's horse came home . . . and there's blood on his coat. These men are going out to search."

Rhonda turned and ran outside to see the horse for herself. When she returned there were tears in her eyes. "Oh, Mother," she sobbed, "he's dead, isn't he? Father's dead!"

Jean took her daughter in her arms and said soothingly, "Now, we don't know that. We've got to have faith that he's only injured. He's not far away. The blood was still moist. These men will find him soon." Seeing that the search party was ready to go, she told the men, "You'll find horses and gear aplenty in the barn—and I deeply appreciate what you're doing for us."

"Our pleasure, ma'am," Clay assured her. "We'll be back as soon as we find your husband."

"Can I have my revolver back?" Fletcher asked him.

"Why should I give it back to you? You pulled it on me once."

"I won't do it again," the saloon owner promised. "I've learned my lesson. I won't be bothering Mrs. LaBonde again." He rubbed his swollen jaw, muttering, "You've convinced me of that."

With some reluctance, Clay reached into his coat pocket and pulled out the nickel-plated revolver. Handing it over, he told Fletcher, "I'm taking you at your word. But if you break it, you're going to regret it." Looking around at the others, Clay asked, "You men all have your guns?"

Each man was equipped.

Clay looked compassionately at Jean and Rhonda Hayes. "You two keep your hopes up, okay?"

"Okay," Jean replied for them both, trying to smile.

Bundled up heavily, the men filed out the back door.

They had been gone from the yard only minutes when Barbara LaBonde and Mattie Phelps came into the kitchen. Jean and Rhonda had a fire going in the cookstove and were about to prepare breakfast. Barbara remarked on seeing the men riding out, and Jean filled her and Mattie in on what was happening.

When breakfast was ready, the four women sat at the table to eat, although Jean and Rhonda picked listlessly at their food. Deciding for Rhonda's sake especially that it would help their spirits to divert their attention from her husband's fate, the rancher's wife engaged the travelers in conversation. "I assume you are a widow, Mrs. Phelps," she said to Mattie.

Mattie answered that she was, and then briefly told the story of her life and the death of her husband some seven years previously. When she had finished, the room again fell silent. Gesturing toward Barbara's unadorned ring finger, Jean asked, "How about you, Mrs. LaBonde? Isn't there a man in your life? I would think someone as lovely as you would have a devoted husband."

Barbara opened up and told the ranch women her whole story, finishing up with Jack's death at the hands of Clay Edwards the previous day. As the brunette wiped away a tear, Jean patted her hand and said, "You've had a pretty rough life, my dear. Maybe things will be better for you now. I'm sure there'll be a man in your future who will love you and give you happiness." Her face brightened, and she asked, "Is Mr. Edwards married?"

"No, he isn't," replied the beautiful woman. "Why do you ask?"

Jean smiled, patted Barbara's hand again, and said, "You just told me about his saving your life when your husband would have killed you, and I saw with my own eyes what he did to that disagreeable Mr. Fletcher for making improper advances. It seems he cares a great deal for you."

"Why, I hardly know him," Barbara protested, showing surprise at such a suggestion.

"I understand," Jean responded, "but when a man does what Mr. Edwards has done for you, he certainly has to care what happens to you. If I were you, I would certainly appreciate him."

"Oh, I do appreciate him," Barbara was quick to reply, "but I don't trust him. Although he appears to be a very kind and unselfish man, experience has taught me to never again trust any man."

After getting directions to the neighboring ranch, the searchers rode through the wintry hush, the only sounds made being crunching snow, puffing horses, and creaking saddles, accompanied by a soft whistling of wind through the pine boughs. Riding two by two, Clay Edwards and Gene Fletcher were in the lead. They were a couple of miles from the ranch when Clay saw movement up ahead. He raised up in the stirrups and squinted against the glare on the snow.

"What you lookin' at, Clay?" asked Claude Overstreet from behind.

"I'm not sure," Clay replied, still peering ahead. "I saw something move a second ago, and—"

"Wolves!" Fletcher gasped, focusing on the same spot. "And there's a man down in the snow!"

Lashing his horse with the reins, Clay jabbed its sides with his heels and rode through the deep snow. There were two male wolves sniffing about the crumpled form in the snow as Clay drew near, yelling, "Heeyah!" The gray canines raised their heads and then bounded away into the thick timber lining the road. Reining in at the spot, with the others coming right behind, Clay leapt from the saddle and stood over the body of the man he assumed was rancher Alan Hayes. The three arrows that had killed him were protruding from his chest.

Overstreet swore as he dismounted and trudged through the snow to Clay. "Indians got him, sure enough!" the driver exclaimed, albeit unnecessarily.

Seconds later all six men stood around the body, looking cautiously in every direction, for hoofprints dotted the area. Clay bent over and began extracting the arrows from the corpse as he remarked, "Those Utes may still be hanging around. Let's put Mr. Hayes on one of the horses and hurry back to the ranch."

"Put him on my horse," suggested Jim McLaughlin. "Len and I can ride double."

Alan Hayes's body was already stiffening from the cold. Working quickly in the frosty air, the men draped the lifeless form over the back of the horse, and the animal nickered and danced about in the snow, reacting to the presence of death.

Gene Fletcher was first in the saddle, ready to ride. While Clay, Overstreet, and Mundy were heading for their mounts, Leonard Robertson swung into his saddle and then extended a hand to his friend, saying, "Come on, Jim. I'll help you up."

Suddenly an arrow hissed out of the nearby timber and struck Len in the neck, plowing all the way through. The startled youth stiffened in the saddle, made a gagging sound, then pitched headfirst into the snow.

Catching a glimpse of the Ute at the edge of the trees, Clay whipped out his gun and fired with blinding speed. The brave slammed backward into a tree from the impact of the slug and slid down to the snow in a sitting position, leaving a trail of blood on the frost-covered bark.

Instantly more arrows whooshed through the air. Terrified, Gene Fletcher dived into the snow and flattened himself in its depths, an arrow burying itself in the saddle where he had been a split second earlier.

Five more Ute warriors were on foot in the shadows of the timber, and the white men dropped to their bellies and opened fire as the arrows flew all around them. As Bill Mundy thumbed back the hammers of his double-barreled shotgun, he spotted a warrior drawing back an arrow in his bow and aiming at Overstreet. The shotgunner raised up to line the twelve-gauge on the Indian and then pulled one trigger. The charge caught the brave in the midsection, blowing a hole so wide it almost cut him in half. Mundy's finger was on the second trigger when another Ute's arrow thwacked into his heart. His finger jerked reflexively, and the second barrel fired as he went down, sending the charge into the trunk of a huge pine.

When the arrow streaked through his friend's neck, Jim McLaughlin quickly drew his revolver and whirled in the direction from which it had come, looking for a target. Spotting the Utes, he fired three times in succession, but he hit nothing. He was about to fire a fourth time when pain lanced through his left side, and he looked down at the arrow that had pierced him at an angle, burying itself two inches deep in his rib cage. He howled and dropped his gun, clutching first at the feathers and then at the point sticking out his back.

Gene Fletcher lay burrowed in the snow, trembling and so terrified that he could not move.

Clay and Overstreet downed braves who were standing beside each other, with the one who took the driver's slug falling on top of the one whom the ex-gunfighter killed.

The two remaining Utes ducked behind trees, conversed for a few seconds, then ran for their ponies, which were standing a few yards deeper in the timber. The determined Edwards jumped to his feet in pursuit, reloading his revolver as he ran. The Indians were vaulting onto their pintos' backs when Clay snapped his gun closed and stopped to take aim. As the Indians bolted away, he drew a bead on the closest one and squeezed the trigger. The revolver bucked against his palm as it roared, and the Ute threw his hands in the air and dropped his bow as he fell onto the snow.

Clay ventured two more shots after the remaining warrior, but he missed, and the Indian got away. The stage driver came puffing up behind and asked, "Did you get 'em?"

"I got one," Clay replied, turning toward Overstreet. "The other one got away."

"That's bad," stated the driver, shaking his head. "He'll probably go after reinforcements."

"No doubt," Clay agreed, breaking open the revolver to reload it again from the gun belt. As they hurried back to the others, he said, "I'm afraid we've got some casualties, Claude."

"Yeah," Overstreet responded, his head drooping and his eyes moist. "Bill was one of 'em."

They reached the battle site to find Gene Fletcher standing over Jim McLaughlin, rifle in hand. The wounded youth lay on his good side, groaning, and Clay ran to him. Overstreet, his face pale, walked slowly to his dead partner, then knelt beside him and began to weep.

Clay looked at Fletcher first and then down at Jim before looking back at Fletcher. Tight-lipped, he asked curtly, "Why don't you help him?"

"I don't know what to do," the thick-bodied man replied weakly.

Clay had glimpsed Fletcher lying motionless in the snow during the battle. Giving him a disgusted look, he snarled, "You didn't know what to do with that rifle either, did you?"

Kneeling beside the wounded teenager, Clay examined the depth and angle of the arrow and said, "You'll be all right, Jim, but I've got to break off the arrow and pull it out. It's going to hurt like you've probably never hurt before, but I'll get it out as quickly as I can."

Jim gritted his teeth and grunted in a pained voice, "Do what you have to."

Clay braced the arrow as best he could and then snapped off the head. Young McLaughlin screamed, and while the scream was still coming, Clay jerked out the arrow. The youth spasmed in agony for a few seconds, then went limp. He had passed out.

Overstreet walked over as Clay was placing Jim's bandanna over the wound. He kept it pressed tightly by unbuckling the youth's gun belt and then rebuckling it higher up. "How is he?" the driver asked softly.

"He'll be all right," Clay replied, closing up Jim's coat. "I'm sure the women at the ranch can patch him up." Reaching under the youth, Clay picked him up. "Let's get going."

Overstreet, looking Gene Fletcher up and down with disdain as they started toward the horses, said, "I didn't hear any firin' goin' on at your post, big fella. Gun jammed?"

Fletcher did not answer.

Clay was a few steps ahead of them. Turning his head to speak over his shoulder, he said bitingly, "His gun wasn't jammed. He was just too busy trying to dig a hole to save his own rotten hide."

Fletcher remained mum, but it was evident that his hatred for Clay Edwards was intensifying.

Placing the bodies on horses, the group headed back for the ranch with a groggy Jim McLaughlin riding double with Clay Edwards. Jean and Rhonda Hayes were grief stricken by the rancher's death, and Barbara and Mattie did what they could to comfort the Hayes women.

Since the ground was frozen too hard for graves to be dug, the rancher's widow instructed the men to place the bodies in the icehouse. Once they were frozen, she would cover them with the sawdust that was used in summer to keep the ice from melting. Come spring she would have neighbors help with the burials.

When the job had been done, the travelers prepared to depart. Barbara LaBonde, who had learned some nursing skills in the past, briefly working for a doctor before her marriage, had stitched and bandaged Jim McLaughlin's side, but it was obvious that the youth was too seriously injured to ride in the coach. Jean insisted that he stay with her and her daughter, saying they would nurse him back to health. As Barbara stepped outside, she turned to Jean. "I have no desire to take my husband's horses," the brunette stated. "Will you keep them?"

The rancher's widow accepted the gift.

Unknown to those at the ranch, the Ute survivor had doubled back and followed the men. He kept watch from a high spot, and when he saw the stagecoach brought out of the barn and made ready for travel, his dark eyes lit up with anticipation. He waited while two women and a stout man climbed inside the coach and two rugged-looking men—one older than the other—climbed onto the seat. The older man took the reins, snapped them, and shouted at the six horses, and when the coach reached the road and headed north, the Ute dashed to his pinto and rode away.

Deep snow and steep grades made it slow going for the Wells Fargo stagecoach. Clay Edwards, sitting in Bill Mundy's seat with a shotgun across his lap, gazed continuously and cautiously around in search of Indians, fully expecting more to show up. His thoughts were on other things as well—specifically, the passengers. Things seemed quiet down in the coach, which relieved Clay, and he hoped that Gene Fletcher would honor his promise to leave Barbara LaBonde alone. Thinking about the captivating woman, Clay wondered why she remained so cool toward him. He found her exciting and very attractive, and she seemed to like him as well, but there was always an invisible wall of defense between them.

The stage pulled into Salida as the sun was setting, and the temperature plunged fast as night fell. The travelers were greatly relieved that no Indian attack had come and that they would spend the night well protected in a town.

Salida's main thoroughfare was three blocks in length and boasted a hotel and three saloons aside from the usual collection of businesses necessary for the existence of a frontier town. Claude Overstreet stopped the coach in front of the Wells Fargo office and made a quick report to the agent of the Indian attack and Bill Mundy's death. Overstreet and his passengers then went to the hotel, and after taking rooms and checking in, they dined together at the hotel's restaurant.

When the meal was over, Gene Fletcher announced to the others, "I noticed on our way into town that the Ram's Head Saloon seems to be the nicest establishment of its kind. I'm going over there for a drink or two, and I'll see you folks in the morning."

The driver frowned and stated, "Don't get drunk, 'cause I don't play nursemaid to passengers who are passed out in their beds. The stage will pull out at sunrise, and if you ain't on it, I ain't gonna come lookin' for you."

Fletcher laughed as he rose from the table and headed for the door. "I'll be up and ready," he called back over his shoulder.

He had been in the Ram's Head for about half an hour, sitting at a table alone, when his attention was drawn to two men at the bar having a dispute. Their voices grew louder and more heated, and Fletcher heard one of the other patrons say that the taller man was Curt Blair. At the mention of the name, the saloon women began withdrawing to a back room, fear showing in their faces, and several of the patrons quickly got up and left. The bartender tried to interrupt the argument, but he was ordered by the men to stay out of it.

Suddenly they faced each other and squared off. One man was short and stocky while the other was six feet tall and thin as a rail. The taller one wore two low-slung guns with fancy pearl handles, and his eyes, peering from under the brim of a black, flat-crowned hat, were chilling.

"Nobody talks like that to me and lives to tell it!" proclaimed the stocky man, his eyes filled with wrath.

"You just met the man who will!" retorted Blair, lowering his splayed hands so they hovered over his gun butts.

The beefy man went for the gun on his hip, but he died on his feet as his opponent drew both guns with lightning speed and drilled him through the heart with two .45-caliber slugs. Blair arrogantly blew the smoke from the muzzles and then dropped them into their holsters.

Several men immediately gathered around him, congratulating him on his prowess. Offhandedly acknowledging them, Blair then turned back to the bar and announced, "Drinks for everybody on me! Curt Blair just killed his tenth man!"

The bartender called for a couple of men to drag the corpse outside. While the remaining patrons were filling their glasses at the expense of the man who apparently was an up-and-coming gunfighter, Gene Fletcher looked

on, wondering where a man got the courage to do what
Blair had just done. The town's marshal entered the saloon and talked to Blair, and after being satisfied that the
duel had been fair, the marshal turned to leave—though
first warning Blair that one day he would meet his match,
and it would be *his* body that was dragged away.

As the lawman pushed through the batwings and
went back out into the cold night, the imperious gunslick
lifted his glass toward the retreating figure and shouted,
"Tin star, you'll be cold in your grave before anybody
drags my body away!"

Watching Blair deal with his fawning admirers, Fletcher
realized that the gunslinger had a burning desire to become famous. The man boasted of his expertise, reeling off
the names of several gunfighters whose reputations he
wanted to match—one of whom was Clay Edwards.

A tingle swept over Fletcher's scalp as an idea came
to him. He figured that Edwards had to be rusty, having
given up gunfighting some two years before, so there was
a good chance that this Blair could outdraw him. And if
Clay Edwards died under Blair's guns, Fletcher could
consider the score he had with the meddlesome ex-
gunfighter to be settled. Smiling, sure that Blair would
welcome the challenge, the traveler stood and threaded
his way over to the slender man. "That was some mighty
fancy shooting, Mr. Blair," he remarked. "I don't think
I've ever seen anyone draw as fast as that."

"Thanks, Mister . . ."

"Fletcher," the husky man replied, smiling.

"I appreciate the compliment. Have a drink on me."

Throwing up a palm, Fletcher said, "No thanks, I've
already had my quota. But . . . let me do *you* a favor."

Blair's cold eyes studied him briefly. "What do you
mean?"

"I just heard you mention Clay Edwards. Did you
know he's been idle for two years? He hasn't drawn a gun
in all that time?"

"Well, I've wondered why I haven't heard anything
about him lately. What's he been doing?"

"Ranching. And his hands are callused and stiff."

"So why are you telling me this?"

Fletcher's voice hardened. "Because I owe the man for something . . . and because he's right here in Salida. Staying over at the hotel. He and I are passengers on the stagecoach that came into town at sunset, and we'll be pulling out at sunrise. He's probably in bed by now, but I'm sure you could call him out when he's boarding the stage in front of the Fargo office in the morning." He chuckled, adding, "The fastest way to become famous is to challenge a man of Edwards's stature and take him down."

A demonic grin spread over Curt Blair's angular face. Cuffing the husky man on the shoulder, he said excitedly, "Thanks, Mr. Fletcher. You'd better tell Edwards goodbye at breakfast, 'cause he won't be around to ride outta here with you."

The Colorado sky was crystal clear as Claude Overstreet drove the stagecoach from the barn in the alley onto the street and parked it in front of the Wells Fargo office. Clay Edwards escorted Barbara LaBonde and Mattie Phelps out of the office into the penetrating cold and opened the coach door for them. Gene Fletcher followed them onto the boardwalk, furtively gazing up and down the street, looking for Curt Blair.

In fact, the gunfighter was directly across the street in the Westerner Café, warming his hands by the wood stove. Seeing people coming out of the Fargo office, Blair hurried to the frost-coated front window and peered out. When he focused on Clay, a smile spread slowly over his thin face, for he recognized the ex-gunfighter from having seen him on two previous occasions. Leaving his heavy coat in the café, Blair stepped outside, crossed the street quickly, and rounded the vehicle.

Clay had just taken hold of the handle used to aid the shotgunner in making his climb to the box when his name was barked: "Edwards!" Having heard that kind of shout before, he knew before turning around that he had a challenger. His holster peeked out from underneath his mackinaw, so there would be little chance of talking his way out of this one.

Several passersby stopped to watch, and Gene Fletcher retraced his steps and stood in the doorway of the Fargo office, a broad grin on his face. Clay took two steps away from the coach and slowly turned around. He did not recognize the beanpole of a man who was staring at him the way a hungry wolf looks at a lamb. Eyeing the man levelly, he said, "You have the advantage over me. I don't know you."

"Yes, you do!" came the instant reply. "I'm Curt Blair! You've heard of me, haven't you?"

"I guess so," Clay responded with a shrug, not wanting to feed the man's confidence too much.

"I'm calling you out, Edwards!" snapped Blair in a voice that said he was feeling sure of the outcome.

"Don't do it," Clay said softly, squaring himself with the man. "I just had breakfast. Don't make it go sour on me for having to kill you."

"I'll give you fifteen seconds to take your gloves off, Edwards," said Blair. "You've now got thirteen left."

The experienced gunfighter had been in this position more times than he cared to remember. The look in Blair's eyes told him the younger man was dead set on his goal. Clay quickly took off his gloves, stuffed them in a coat pocket, and moved toward the center of the snow-covered street, saying, "Okay, let's get this over with."

Blair sneered and flexed his fingers against the cold, lining himself some forty feet from the man he intended to kill. Lowering his hands over his guns, he curled them expectantly. There was a moment of utter stillness, then Blair's hands dropped.

It was over in less than a heartbeat. Clay's weapon seemed to leap into his hand, firing before Curt Blair's guns cleared leather. The bullet exploded Blair's heart, and its impact flattened him on his back in the snow. There was a look of shock on his face, and his unseeing eyes seemed ready to pop from their sockets.

Salida's marshal stepped into the street and stood over Blair, shaking his head. When Clay walked over to him, the marshal remarked, "I told him just last night that one day he would meet his match. Looks like that day came sooner than either one of us expected—especially him."

Holstering his gun, Clay pivoted and returned to the coach. Climbing up beside the driver, he said, "Let's go, Claude."

Overstreet looked over his shoulder at Gene Fletcher, who stood as if rooted in the doorway of the Fargo office, and called, "Fletcher, you comin' with us?"

The husky man blinked, rubbed a gloved hand over his eyes, and climbed into the coach. As the frost-covered vehicle rolled out of Salida, Fletcher looked back to see someone dragging Curt Blair's body off the street.

Chapter Nine

Clay Edwards sat up on the box, taking in the awesome, rugged country around him as Salida passed from view. Vast expanses of unbroken white blanketed meadows and forests, filled gorges and ravines, and swept up mountainsides to their sawtoothed peaks. The crisp air was icy cold, but it was also invigorating—and it was good to be alive.

As Clay breathed deeply, he thought of Curt Blair, lying on the undertaker's table by now, with rigor mortis already beginning to stiffen his body. If the cocky upstart had only taken the warning, he could be breathing this same fresh air. Clay briefly considered taking off the revolver strapped to his hip, thereby avoiding another such inevitable confrontation. But then he considered the Utes and realized that he had to be well-prepared to fight the Indians if they attacked. No, he told himself, you can't take off the gun until there's no more chance of Indian trouble.

As the sun rose higher, the wind began to rush down off the high peaks, knifing its way through the coats worn by the driver and his replacement shotgun guard. Claude Overstreet cursed the wind, pulling his hat down tighter and his collar up higher. Clay held the shotgun between his knees, beat his gloved hands together, and swung his arms to restore circulation.

An hour after leaving Salida, the coach was making a mile-long climb up the side of a mountain through eighteen or so inches of snow. Hunched into their harness, the horses had their heads bent low, struggling to haul the vehicle up the steep incline.

Inside the coach Gene Fletcher huddled in his blanket, letting his eyes rest on Barbara LaBonde's beautiful face. The brunette and Mattie Phelps leaned against each other, their eyes closed. The saloon owner's thoughts strayed to the gunfight, and Fletcher pictured it over and over, wondering how Clay could be so fast after two years of not using a gun. Angered at the way his plan had gone awry, he told himself he would find another way to get Clay Edwards killed.

With the coach angled so steeply, Fletcher had to brace his feet hard against the floor to keep from sliding off his rear-facing seat onto the two women. While shifting a foot for a better hold, he bumped Barbara's leg. She stirred, opened her eyes, and sat up straight. Mattie was sound asleep, and her limp form remained against Barbara's shoulder. Barbara's eyes met Fletcher's, and he was watching her hungrily. She gave him a stern scowl and looked away.

Fletcher smiled and said, "I promised Edwards I wouldn't bother you anymore during this trip, but how about if I ride over to Aspen come spring and see you?"

Vexation was evident on Barbara's face. Her blue eyes flashed as she retorted loudly, "Do you have a hearing problem, Mr. Fletcher? How many times do I have to tell you that you do not interest me? I have a strong aversion toward men in general, but I positively loathe you! When this horrible trip is over, I never want to lay eyes on you again! I hope this time I have made myself clear!"

Fletcher did not reply. A sullen look settled over his face, and he pushed back the leather curtain and stared outside.

The coach was still halfway from the crest when Claude Overstreet turned to the man beside him and said, "Clay, the horses are givin' it all they got, but we're gonna have to give 'em help. Would you mind gettin' Fletcher, and each of you take a rear wheel? If you two big strong fellas could help roll the wheels forward, it would ease the load on the team."

Laying the shotgun on the floor of the box, Clay said, "Sure," and after Overstreet pulled rein, the ex-gunfighter dropped to the ground. Walking to the door, he pulled it open and said, "Come on, Fletcher. You and I have to give the team some help. You take the rear wheel on this side. I'll take the other one. Grab a spoke when it's even with your knees and give it a hoist till it's vertical. Just keep doing that till we reach the top."

Fletcher started to balk but then relented. Muttering, he reluctantly threw aside the blanket and stepped out of the coach. Barbara removed her blanket and started to climb out behind Fletcher, but Clay told her, "You don't need to get out, Mrs. LaBonde. You don't weigh enough to make that much difference. Mrs. Phelps, that goes for you, too," he added, addressing the elderly woman who sat rubbing the sleep from her eyes.

Ignoring the suggestion, Barbara climbed down into the snow, insisting, "I'm not getting out just to lighten the load. I want to help push."

"Now, ma'am," Clay countered, "we can't be letting you do that. You might hurt yourself. This kind of thing is a man's work."

"I can handle it, I assure you," she said crisply. "I was raised doing hard work. It fell upon my sister and me to take over the work on our place when my father and my brothers were out drinking and carousing. Come on. Let's get this vehicle over the mountain."

Overstreet handled the reins, the two men worked at the wheels, and Barbara braced her back against the stagecoach at the rear and pushed. It was slow going, but they finally reached the crest, and while his passengers and team were catching their breath, the driver leapt from the box and trudged ahead to take a look down the other side. Walking back to where the others stood, he said, "Gonna be touchy goin' down."

"Why's that?" queried Clay, panting.

Overstreet beat his hands together to warm them and said, "Looks like the wind must've blown awful hard on that side of the mountain when it was snowin', and it sorta gullied out the road. The snow ain't deep like we just came through, but there's an icy crust on the surface that looks mighty slick." Chuckling, he added, "Might have to ask all of you to drag your feet to help hold 'er back on the way down."

Mattie gasped, and Overstreet turned and looked at the ashen face peering at him from the window. "Just kiddin', ma'am," he assured her. "It'll be all right." Then, to the others, he said, "Rest time's over. Let's move."

Clay gave Barbara his hand and helped her in, but he stretched his arm across the door as Fletcher started to follow her. The husky man stopped short, frowned, and demanded, "What's this?"

There was a warning note in Clay's voice as he eyed the man levelly and said, "I heard the lady's rebuke a short while ago. I thought we had an agreement."

Fear was evident in Fletcher's eyes. "Now, look, Edwards," he protested meekly, "I was only talking. I didn't realize that what I was saying would upset her."

Clay looked at Barbara, who was shaking her head, and then he ordered the thick-bodied man, "You're going to ride shotgun for a while, and I'll ride down here. Up in the box you'll not be saying things that upset the lady." Gesturing to the seat, he said, "The shotgun's on the floor. You know how to use one?"

Fletcher said tersely, "Yeah."

"Will you use it if you have to?"

Glaring at Clay, Gene Fletcher nodded crisply and said, "Don't worry. I'll use it."

When Fletcher was seated up top and Clay was seated in the coach, Overstreet eased the vehicle over the crest and headed down the precipitous, ice-encrusted road. The horses had to dig their hooves in hard, and the driver had to hold back on the brake to keep the vehicle from going

too fast. From the corner of his eye the driver could see
that Fletcher was gripping the seat and bracing his feet,
terrified and oblivious to the cold wind lashing his face.
Overstreet understood the man's fear: The path in front of
them was so steep, it looked almost vertical.

The coach was about a hundred yards past the crest
when it approached a level area laden with dense forest off
to the right. Suddenly a band of whooping, screeching
Utes came thundering out of the trees toward the coach,
firing rifles. A bullet hummed past Overstreet's head, and
he bawled, "Use the shotgun, Fletcher! I've got my hands
full!"

Still bracing his feet against the tilt of the vehicle,
Fletcher shakily hoisted the double-barreled twelve-gauge
shotgun and thumbed back the hammers. As he was bringing the heavy weapon up and lining it on one of the
Indians, a bullet struck him high in the chest, but the
shotgun roared and the Indian took the smoking charge in
the neck, just below his chin. While the Ute sailed off the
horse's back, blood spurting, Fletcher collapsed on the
seat, gripping the rail in agony. The shotgun, with one
hammer still cocked, leaned against his legs.

Inside the coach, as he reached for the Winchester
repeater that Overstreet had given him, Clay Edwards
shouted at the women to get down on the floor. Jacking a
cartridge into the chamber, he leaned out the window on
the right side and started firing. The howling Indians were
circling around to the rear of the stage, and on his third
shot Clay knocked one of them off his pinto.

Bullets chewed into the coach, and Mattie Phelps
cried out something unintelligible. Claude Overstreet let
go of the brake handle, grabbed the reins with his left
hand, and drew his pistol with his right. The frightened
team began picking up speed, and the coach immediately
began bounding down the steep decline. The Utes were
momentarily left behind but then came on the run, firing
their rifles.

Clay leaned out the coach window and fired rapidly at

the pursuing warriors, but the bouncing of the vehicle made his shots miss their marks. Barbara LaBonde reached for the other Winchester, which Overstreet had earlier given Fletcher. She picked it up from the floor, worked the lever, and leaned out the window on the opposite side of the coach from Clay. Hearing Barbara firing, Clay paused in his own shooting and shouted, "Mrs. LaBonde! Get your head inside and get down!"

Barbara kept on firing as she called back over her shoulder, "No sense having an idle gun!"

Suddenly one of the team took a bullet in the rump and bolted, frightening the others, and they began thundering down the mountain road at breakneck speed. Overstreet holstered his gun and yanked on the reins with both hands, but his efforts to control the horses were useless. The coach, swaying dangerously, careened and skidded, and the Utes pulled back and waited for the inevitable.

Despite his wound, Gene Fletcher managed to hold onto the rail, frozen with terror. Claude Overstreet desperately tried to rein in the team, but though the snaffles bit deep into the horses' mouths, it made no difference. The animals were charging down the mountain in a blind frenzy.

Clay Edwards threw aside his rifle and lunged across a screaming Mattie Phelps. Grasping both her and Barbara, he pulled them down, shouting, "We're going to crash!" As he spoke, he wrapped his arms around the brunette and placed himself between her and the front of the coach, ready to use his body to cushion her against the coming impact.

The terror-blinded horses headed straight for the trees. Suddenly the wounded one collapsed in the harness, causing the others to stumble, and the team became a mass of scrambling legs and flying hooves. Up top, Claude Overstreet watched like a man hypnotized. His senses returned to him just before the impact, and he leapt off the box and clear of the coach. Immediately after, the fishtailing coach slammed into a huge pine, smashing one side and then flipping over before coming to rest with two wheels spinning ceaselessly. The harness broke, and four of the terrified horses galloped into the trees and disappeared; the remaining two were down with broken legs.

Hitting the snow face first, Overstreet lay stunned. Gene Fletcher was thrown into the tree upon impact and killed. Inside the coach Mattie Phelps was dead of a broken neck, her crumpled body lying in a corner next to the coach's roof, which was almost completely torn off. Clay held Barbara tightly in his powerful arms, and ignoring the pain shooting through his right leg, he asked her, "Are you all right?"

Gasping for breath, her head against his chest, she replied, "Yes . . . yes, I think so." She looked over at the elderly woman and tears filled her eyes. "Poor old thing," she breathed.

Clay released his hold so Barbara could crawl off him, and then he reached for his rifle. "Stay here," he whispered. "Those Indians will be down on us any minute. I have no idea what's happened to Overstreet or Fletcher."

Pulling his legs up under him, he grimaced. Then he stood and pushed the door of the coach open.

"Are you hurt?" Barbara asked with concern.

"I think my leg's broken," he replied as he cautiously rose up through the opening, rifle ready.

"What do you see?" inquired Barbara.

"Claude's lying in the snow about thirty feet away, but he's moving a bit. Fletcher seems to be dead, but—" He broke off at the sight of four Utes coming toward the coach, rifles raised over their heads. They were looking directly at him and were no more than sixty yards away. "Indians are coming!" he told Barbara. "Stay down, but find the other rifle if you can. If they get me, play dead. Should one of them try to climb in here to check, shoot him."

Suddenly Overstreet rolled over and sat up, looking around as though trying to get his bearings. "Claude!"

Clay called. "The Utes are coming for us! Can you get to the coach?"

Overstreet focused on Clay and started to reply when the warriors reached the bottom of the steep decline. Whooping and shouting their war cry, ready for the kill, they put their horses to a gallop. Clay raised his rifle and took aim at the Indian in the lead, but he inadvertently put weight on his right leg. The pain that spiraled through the leg made him wince just as he pulled the trigger, and the bullet whizzed over the Indian's head. Moaning and bracing himself on his left leg, he worked the lever and fired again. He hit the third Ute in the line, knocking him from the pinto's back.

Claude Overstreet was on his knees with his revolver aimed at the charging Indians. He fired, hitting the lead Ute, but the other two were right on top of him, shooting their single-shot rifles point-blank. The rugged driver flopped to his back in the snow with his heart ripped by two slugs.

Lining the Winchester on another Indian, Clay drilled him through the head. The remaining warrior sat his dancing horse, frantically searching his fur breeches for another bullet. Clay worked the lever of his rifle, took quick aim, and squeezed the trigger—but the hammer came down with an empty, hollow sound. Hearing it, the Indian dropped his rifle and leapt from his horse. He plowed through the snow as fast as he could, screeching wildly and drawing a long-bladed knife.

Clay let the empty rifle slip from his fingers and clawed for the revolver on his hip. The holster was empty. Pain lanced through him as he dropped down and frantically asked Barbara, "Do you see my revolver anywhere?"

Desperately Barbara looked around and replied, "No! I can't find the other rifle, either! Maybe they fell outside when we turned over!"

Despite the pain, Clay knew he had no choice but to fight hand to hand, and he climbed hurriedly through the door opening to meet the approaching Ute. Timing his move, he dived off the coach, landing on the Indian with the full force of his weight. The two men rolled in the snow, thrashing about in a fight to the death. Clay's right leg felt as though it were on fire, but he forced the pain from his mind as he grabbed the Indian's wrist just in time to prevent the knife from being plunged into his chest. Again they rolled, each trying to overcome the other, and when they slammed against a tree, the Ute was on top, bearing down with his knife and determined to kill the white man.

They met each other strength for strength. When Clay smashed the Indian's knife hand violently against the rough bark of the tree, the Ute howled as the skin peeled off. Clay repeatedly slammed the bleeding hand against the trunk, until finally the knife flew out of his enemy's grasp and was buried in the deep snow.

Enraged, the Indian screamed and tried to pound Clay in the face, but the more muscular cowboy fended the Ute off with his elbows and then rolled away from the tree, throwing his enemy into the snow. Instantly both men were on their feet and began trading blows. At first one combatant seemed to be the victor, but then the tide turned in favor of the other.

The agony of his injured leg was beginning to drain the strength from Clay's body. He knew he had to finish the Indian off quickly or the fight would end with his own death. Abruptly the Ute leapt to the spot where he had seen his knife plunge into the snow, and he pawed through the cold, white mantle, trying frantically to find the weapon. Desperate to best the Indian before his strength waned, Clay tackled him and sank his strong fingers into the warrior's long hair, shoving his face into the snow. The Ute sputtered and fought to free himself before he suffocated, but the white man was too strong. Drawing from his reserves of energy, Clay held his adversary's face down until the Indian ceased to struggle. Panting for breath himself, he held the man there another thirty seconds. When he was certain the Ute was dead, he let go and rose to his feet.

Turning toward the wreckage of the coach, Clay saw Barbara LaBonde watching him, eyes wide. With the breath sawing in and out of him, he weakly gasped, "It—It's okay. You . . . can come out . . . now." Then his knees gave way, and he collapsed in the snow. His head began to spin, a blackness overcame him, and he passed out.

Barbara climbed out of the coach, first slogging through the snow to the driver to grab Overstreet's revolver and shoving it into her pocket, just in case. Averting her gaze from Gene Fletcher's body—and feeling a twinge of guilt for not caring that he was dead—she hurried to Clay's side. She knelt down beside the unconscious man and pulled up the right leg of his pants to examine his injury.

Barbara's nursing experience had taught her much about broken bones, and she recognized the fracture immediately. It would have to be set, and since Clay was already unconscious, it was the perfect opportunity to do it. Running her experienced fingers up and down the leg from the knee to the ankle to get the exact picture of separation in her mind, she set it quickly. The unconscious man moaned softly but did not come to.

Working fast to bind the leg before Clay came around, she used broken pieces of floorboard from the coach as splints, and cloth from Mattie Phelps's dress to tie them in place. When that was done, she rose and looked around, taking a deep breath. Dark clouds were gathering in the west and the wind was picking up. The young woman told herself that she and Clay Edwards were in a serious predicament. There had to be more Indians somewhere near, and it looked as though the weather would turn bad—and there was no shelter in sight. It was going to be up to her to get them out of their dilemma.

Trudging back to the stagecoach, Barbara examined the wreckage. She then tested the loosened roof of the vehicle and found that with a single tug on the metal rack it severed from the frame. Perfect, she thought. Not much different than a toboggan! Taking the ropes that had lashed the luggage to the rack, she tied them to one end and pulled the makeshift sled to where Clay Edwards lay in the snow, greatly relieved that it glided easily. With some effort, she rolled his muscular body onto the sled, laying him on his back.

That done, she steeled herself and went to put the two injured horses out of their misery. She collected herself after shooting the animals and then busily gathered other essentials scattered in and about the stagecoach, packing much of it into Gene Fletcher's travel bag: both Winchester repeaters, several boxes of ammunition, a tin cup, matches, a coach lantern, the buffalo-hide blankets, and some beef jerky—what little she could find. Apparently, the bulk of the food as well as the canteens had been thrown out of the coach and lost in the snow, or they were buried under the wreckage. She also retrieved her own bag and took a few moments to pile on additional layers of clothes under her coat.

After making several trips back and forth to the sled, she returned a final time and found that Clay had come to. He was staring at the sky with pain-filled eyes, and it was clear that his leg was hurting severely. Hearing her footsteps crunching in the snow, he wiped a hand over his face and raised up on his elbows.

"So, you came back finally," she said softly, placing the last load on the sled.

"What are you doing, ma'am?" he asked, bewildered.

Reaching in a pocket of her coat, Barbara handed him the revolver he had lost when the stage crashed. Finally she replied, "Getting ready to travel."

Shoving the gun in its holster, he questioned, "Are you planning to pull this thing?"

"Have to," she confirmed. "The Indian ponies all took off, as did four of the team. The other two had broken legs. I shot them."

Clay looked at his own splinted leg. "What about me?"

"Your leg's broken, too, but I decided not to shoot you," Barbara said evenly.

Clay grinned at her touch of humor at such a serious moment, then asked, "How do you know it's broken?"

"I've dealt with lots of broken bones. Take my word for it . . . it's broken between the knee and the ankle. I set it. It should be all right in a few weeks if you stay off it."

Clay laid his head back and sighed. After a few seconds he looked up at the beautiful woman and said, "Ma'am, you can't pull this thing with me on it."

"Have to," she repeated. "More Indians could show up, so we've got to find a safe place as soon as possible. I'm going to head us north and pull in at the first ranch we come to."

"But my weight will be too much for you," Clay argued. "Maybe I can make a crutch and—"

"You've got to stay completely off the leg, Mr. Edwards," Barbara cut in. "I'll pull the sled." She paused, then added, "I hate leaving Mattie's and Claude's bodies, but we have to concern ourselves with our survival, and every minute counts."

She reached over, pulled out two buffalo robes, and covered Clay with them. "You need to keep that leg warm, too."

Clay smiled gratefully, but she ignored it.

Moving to the front of the sled, Barbara stepped into the looped rope and lifted it to her midsection. Bowing against the weight behind her, she dug her booted feet into the snow and started northward. Looking up at the sky, now filled with dark, ominous clouds, and feeling the wind beginning to blow harder, Barbara prayed that she would have the physical and spiritual strength needed to bring them to safety.

Chapter Ten

The icy wind howled over the snow-covered mountains as Barbara LaBonde pulled the makeshift sled across the frozen, slippery crust on the road, pressing northward. The sled glided relatively easily at first, but soon the snow began getting deeper, since the wind had only cleaned off the road on the steep decline and for a short distance after it bottomed out.

Now they were climbing again, and in snow over a foot deep. Straining every muscle, Barbara plodded and pulled. Clay Edwards lay under the buffalo-hide blankets and watched her, astonished at her determination as well as her gallantry. She could easily have walked away on her own and found safety for herself, but instead she was expending her strength to the limit, laboring to haul *him* to safety as well. However, it bothered the big muscular man to be in such a position; he should be the one helping her, not vice versa.

Soon the road got steeper and the snow got deeper. Her breath visible in the frosty air as she exerted herself, Barbara leaned into the rope. Often her feet slipped, but she struggled to find solid footing and then continued on. After about half an hour the young woman dropped to her knees, exhausted.

Clay sat up and stated, "Mrs. LaBonde, you can't keep this up. It's just too much for you."

Looking over her shoulder and gasping hard for air,

Barbara rejoined, "I . . . have to . . . Mr. Edwards. There is . . . no other . . . alternative."

"But there is," he countered. "Or rather, there are. First off, I can make myself some crutches and take the bulk of the weight off the sled by walking. If I find that I can't do it, the second option is that you leave me and go on alone. Find shelter for yourself."

"I'm not going to leave you," she said emphatically, her voice now firm. "That leg must be examined by a doctor if at all possible. I think I set it right, but it really needs to be checked by someone who can say for sure. If I can find a ranch, someone there can ride to the nearest doctor and bring him."

"I appreciate your concern for me very much, ma'am," said Clay, throwing the blankets off and sitting up. "But I can't let you keep pulling my weight. Let's find a fallen tree and see if we can break off a branch and make me a set of crutches."

She shrugged. "I can see there's no use in arguing with you. You'll have to find out for yourself." Looking around, she pointed to a fallen birch tree a few feet off the road that had some limbs protruding from the snow.

"That should do just fine," Clay remarked. "Could you pull the sled close to it so I can get hold of the branches?"

Barbara complied, and after a brief struggle he was able to break off a Y-shaped limb thick enough to serve as a crutch. Determined to alleviate her burden, he worked his way to his feet and leaned on the limb, but he experienced severe pain with just the slightest weight on the leg. He then broke off another limb of similar length and thickness, using it as a second crutch and enabling him to keep the right foot elevated.

Shaking her head as they continued upward, Barbara let Clay take the lead while she followed, pulling the sled, which was now much lighter. The big muscular man had regained some energy while lying down, and he was moving well at the moment. But Barbara knew that his strength was almost totally spent from fighting the Indian, and the pain of the injury itself had drained off what was left. He would not make it a hundred yards.

The young widow was right. Clay had managed to hobble through the snow for about sixty yards before he collapsed and passed out. Though weary herself Barbara rolled the unconscious man onto the sled, covered him with the buffalo blankets, and started onward again, slowly dragging him higher up the road.

As Barbara pressed on, snow began to fall, swirled about by the wind. The flakes were big and fat, silent forerunners of the lengthy snow to come. Puffing and straining, the valiant woman thought about taking the injured man back to Salida but soon dismissed the idea. She could never manage to haul him that far. The only thing she could do was keep moving north in hopes of finding a ranch where they could get help.

Worry was scratching at the back of her mind. When the Utes in the area found their dead comrades, they would come looking for the survivors of the coach wreck with vengeance on their minds. She must find a place of safety soon. The worry became stronger as Barbara felt her body protesting and her strength waning. How much longer could she keep up the struggle?

When Clay Edwards regained consciousness, his senses returned slowly. He was first aware of the howling wind, and then he felt the thick snowflakes. The slant of the sled told him they were on a very steep slope, but there was no sense of motion, which meant they were stopped. Suddenly he became cognizant of another sound above the whine of the wind: Barbara LaBonde was weeping.

Rising up on his elbows, Clay saw her down on her knees in the snow, the rope around her waist stretched tight. Even in her exhaustion she was keeping the toboggan from sliding back down the slope. Clearing his throat, Clay said, "Ma'am . . ."

Barbara's weeping subsided. She looked around, her

face wet with tears, and said, "I'm glad you're awake. Are you all right?"

"I'm fine, thanks to you, ma'am," he replied tenderly. "But I've got to do something to alleviate the strain on you."

"You've already discovered there's nothing you can do," she responded, sniffing and wiping tears with the back of her gloved hand. "I'm just so afraid more Utes are going to show up."

Noting the force of the snow, he remarked, "If this storm turns out to be as severe as it seems it will, it could delay a scouting party and give us time to escape."

"I hope so," she said wearily, rising to her feet. "I can face just about anything except those bloody savages."

A wave of helplessness mixed with guilt washed over the ex-gunfighter as the brunette leaned into the rope and began hauling the sled farther upward. He hated the situation and wished it away, but the snow kept falling, the wind kept blowing, and Barbara kept climbing.

After twenty minutes the young woman dropped into the snow, gulping for breath. Clay sat up and said, "Mrs. LaBonde, you've got to rest." He peered through the snow and then exclaimed, "Look over there! There's a boulder surrounded by fir trees. If we can get on the lee side of it, you can wrap yourself in one of these blankets and at least be out of the wind."

Without waiting for a response, Clay rolled off the sled and began dragging himself toward the relative shelter with his hands. Barbara struggled to her feet and followed, pulling the sled. When they were settled in a protected spot, the exhausted woman curled up inside a buffalo-hide robe and leaned against the boulder. Pulling himself back onto the sled, Clay wrapped himself in the other robe. When Barbara's breathing returned to normal, he commented, "Ma'am, I overheard what you said to Fletcher this morning. Do you really hate men as much as you say?"

Nodding sharply, she replied, "Yes, I do."

"Well, then, you've got me a bit puzzled. Why are you helping me?"

"You saved my life twice, so I owe you," came the matter-of-fact reply.

"You don't owe me anything, ma'am," he said quietly. "I only did what had to be done when the situation demanded it."

Barbara's expression softened. Lowering her barrier a bit, she replied, "I know it was more than that, Mr. Edwards. You could have gotten yourself shot when you kept Jack from killing me. And just before we crashed, you had to choose between cushioning me or Mattie. You chose me. If you hadn't, I would have been the one to die. I don't know why you made that decision, but as sorry as I am that the poor old thing didn't make it, I love life and am grateful that you did what you did."

Clay wanted to tell her that since he could protect only one of them, he had chosen Barbara because she was doing strange things to his heart—but he kept it to himself. Instead he said, "My reflexes just aimed me toward you, ma'am."

Barbara smiled slightly. "It was more than reflexes that made you want to cushion *anybody*, Mr. Edwards. You could have tried to find a way to protect yourself— and perhaps you wouldn't have ended up with a broken leg. You are a very kind and unselfish person."

Wishing to steer the conversation away from himself, Clay said, "Speaking of your husband, ma'am, I want you to know that I'm very sorry you were so mistreated by him. I just don't understand how a man could treat a woman so poorly."

"The world's full of men just like him," she countered, her cynicism evident.

"Well," he said, trying to encourage her, "you're young and very beautiful. You can still know happiness when you find the right man—one who'll genuinely love you and provide for you."

Through clenched teeth she snapped, "There is no

such man! They'll court you and tell you sweet, loving lies, but then they'll turn out to be just like Jack, my father, and my two no-good brothers!"

Barbara's anger gave her the added strength she needed. Leaping to her feet, she flung off the heavy hide blanket and dumped it on top of Clay. Stepping into the loop of the rope, she said briskly, "We have a lot more ground to cover," and hauled the sled back to the road.

The temperature was dropping, and the wind periodically whipped the falling snow, but the plucky woman continued on. Clay studied Barbara as she dragged him northward through the storm, thinking about her bitterness toward her father and brothers. Clearly she must have seen a great deal of the same thing after marrying Jack LaBonde that she had within her family. So no doubt she had good reason to be bitter and to distrust men. He wondered if she would ever give anyone the chance to change her mind, the chance to show her what real happiness could be like with someone who truly loved her.

Barbara had to rest a number of times, but she called on her deepest reserves and kept a steady pace northward for nearly three hours. They had just crested the top of a long hill and had stopped so she could rest, when she gasped.

Clay sat up as he saw the terror on her face. "What is it?" he asked.

"Indians!" she replied, pointing to a spot below them.

Following her finger, Clay saw a band of Utes on a lower level, looking like ghostly wraiths in the swirling snow, moving in their direction. Palming both revolvers—his own and the one Barbara had taken from Claude Overstreet's body—he stated, "I think they must know we're up here. We're going to have to take a stand."

There was defeat in Barbara's eyes. Grimly she said, "Mr. Edwards, we don't have a chance against eight Indians."

"We can't give up, ma'am," countered the ex-gunfighter. "I know the burden is on you, but if we can get into the timber quickly, we might be able to lose them before they get up here. The snow is coming down hard enough to cover our tracks in a matter of minutes."

Clay's words seemed to give the young woman renewed hope. Nodding, she said, "Let's give it a try."

Lunging into the snow and breathing hard, Barbara dragged the sled up a slight slope into the dense timber. The wind and snow combined covered their tracks almost as soon as they made them. When Barbara's strength gave out, she fell to her knees. She and Clay looked back toward the road, and through the trees and a curtain of blowing snow they watched the Utes guide their horses by the spot where they had left the road ten minutes before. The snow-covered warriors leaned from their mounts, looking for telltale signs, and soon passed from view.

"Whew!" breathed Barbara. "I never thought I would be thankful for a snowstorm!"

"A blessing and a curse at the same time," remarked Clay. Looking up, he mused, "It's hard to tell exactly without the sun, but it must be late afternoon. If we don't find some shelter and warmth by dark, we could freeze to death. At this altitude, the temperature will plummet when night falls."

Barbara nodded solemnly. "I guess the only thing we can do is stay in the timber and keep moving. We sure had better not go back to the road, in case those Utes return."

"You're right about that," agreed Clay, holstering his revolver and placing the other one next to his left leg under the blanket.

After eating a bit of beef jerky and hardtack to keep up their strength, they moved on. Soon they were climbing higher in the timber through the blinding storm.

About a half hour later they stopped so Barbara could rest. She was on her knees in the snow, gasping for breath, when suddenly the air was split by two rapid gunshots, followed by the roar of a wild animal. Clay and Barbara stared briefly at each other and then turned their heads in the direction the sounds had come from. There was another roar, several more shots, and then a pause and another pair of shots.

When once again there was nothing but the howl of the wind, Barbara asked, "What do you make of it?"

"I'd say it's someone with a shotgun—probably a hunter, and a bear," Clay replied. "A very large bear."

Swinging her arms to keep warm, she remarked, "Correct me if I'm wrong, but aren't bears in hibernation by now?"

Clay replied, "Yes, but bears always hibernate in caves, and sometimes hunters will sneak in and shoot a beast while it's asleep. Unless you can put a bullet directly into the bear's heart, or through its brain, it'll take more than one shot to kill it—and from what we just heard, I would say it took six slugs to do the job."

Barbara nodded absently and then glanced up at the leaden sky. "It looks to me like we're beginning to lose light already. We'd better get moving again."

"I think the shots came from over that way," Clay said, pointing. "Let's head in that direction. With luck, we'll find those hunters—and their cabin."

"Start praying, Mr. Edwards," Barbara replied, getting to her feet. Wind and snow buffeted her as she pressed through the timber, mustering all the strength she could. In an effort to ward off the punishing elements, she bent her head as far as she could and still see where she was going.

Time passed, and darkness began to close in around the travelers. Barbara was about to stop for another brief rest when Clay raised his voice above the howl of the wind and shouted, "Mrs. LaBonde! Look!"

Barbara halted, wiping the crystals of ice clinging to her eyelashes, and turned around to look at him. He was pointing through the woods off to his right.

"Over there! A cave! Do you see it?"

Swinging her gaze to where he pointed, Barbara saw the dark yawning mouth of a large cave. Relief washed over her. Now they had a place to get out of the storm for the night. "I see it!" she said excitedly. New energy rushed through her weary body, and she lunged into the rope. When they were within twenty yards of the cave, a ghastly thought raced into Barbara's mind. Stopping short, she whirled around and said, "Mr. Edwards, what if there are bears in the cave?"

Clay chuckled. "Then we'll be real quiet so we don't wake them up!"

The small joke relieved Barbara's anxiety, and she smiled. As she started forward again, Clay shouted, "I'll paddle with my hands!"

Digging his hands into the snow to help propel the sled forward, Clay pushed rapidly with all his might. Minutes later Barbara stepped into the black maw of the cave, hauling the sled in behind her. She was completely exhausted, and her hands and feet were nearly numb from the cold.

Clay already had the coach lamp out and ready, and he struck a match and lit the wick. A warm yellow glow immediately filled the mouth of the cave. Handing Barbara the lamp, he said, "Looks like the cave turns to the right back there. If you'll allow me to lean on your shoulder for support, I'll hold one of these rifles ready, and we'll see what's around the corner."

Working their way slowly toward the back wall of the cave, the couple found that beyond the bend the relatively spacious cave extended for another twenty feet. To their surprise and delight, they found cut wood stacked in a corner, evidence that hunters had used the cave. The travelers would have a fire, and by staying at the far end of the cave, they would be away from the icy blades of the wind.

Sitting on the dirt floor with his splinted leg extended stiffly from his body, Clay built a fire near the bend, placing it so the smoke would be drawn out the opening, yet heat would be thrown to the back of the cave.

Within minutes the fire was blazing. Sitting close to

it, Clay and Barbara opened their coats, welcoming the warmth, and began to thaw out. Barbara sighed with relief and remarked, "We've got enough jerky and hardtack to make a meal tonight, but there'll be no breakfast in the morning."

"I won't eat anything," he replied. "You eat half tonight and have the other half tomorrow. You've done all the work, so you need to replenish your strength. Perhaps if it stops snowing tonight I can use my crutches in the morning and hopefully find some small game running around out there. If so, we'll have fresh meat to eat tomorrow."

Barbara tried to convince him to eat some of the meager provisions, but he refused. Reluctantly she ate some food in front of him, and then they used the tin cup to melt snow for water. Comfortably warm, they leaned back against the wall of the cave, watched the fire burn, and listened to the wind howl.

Neither had spoken for some time when Clay said, "I sort of wish there had been a bear in here."

Eyes wide, Barbara looked at him aghast. "Why on earth would you wish that?"

"I could have shot it, and we would've had plenty of meat to eat."

Barbara laid her back against the rough stone and laughed. "Well, it sounds good in theory, but if you had missed his heart or his brain, it might have been the bear that had plenty of meat to eat—you and me!"

Clay laughed with her, and then they both fell silent again. After a couple of minutes he looked at her and said, "You're quite a woman, Mrs. LaBonde."

Meeting his gaze, Barbara asked dryly, "You mean because I've hauled you over these mountains in a snowstorm?"

Nodding, he responded, "That, and what I know of your past."

Barbara shrugged. "I'm no different than other women."

"Yes, you are. You've got grit. I admire a woman with

grit. Many women who are beautiful and feminine are like delicate china dolls—they break under the least bit of pressure. You've got all the beauty and femininity a man could ever want in a woman, but it's the grit that makes you special."

Barbara did not reply. She looked back at the fire. As the shadows from the dancing flames flickered on her exquisite features, Clay Edwards felt his heart beating fast. If only she did not have such a strong aversion toward men . . .

After a few moments he mused, "Whoever they are who fired those shots we heard have to be camped or housed somewhere near. If we can find them, our wanderings may be over."

"I hope so," she replied. "As soon as I know you're in good hands with that leg, I've got to find a way to get to Aspen."

"We'll see what morning brings," Clay suggested. "Right now, I guess we'd better turn in. We'll need to wrap up good in these buffalo blankets. When the fire goes out, it'll get cold in here."

The next morning was cold, windy, and cloudy, but the snow had stopped falling. After building a fire, Clay told Barbara to eat the remainder of the hardtack and jerky while he went hunting for small game. Struggling with his crude crutches, he tucked a rifle under his arm and left the cave.

As he hobbled his way through the deep snow, he squinted against the dull glare, searching the ground for sign of squirrels or rabbits. He was about fifty yards from the cave when he saw tendrils of smoke lifting above the timber at a spot about a half mile below. Hope rising, he quickly shifted position so he could locate the source of the smoke. Suddenly he saw it: a log cabin, smoke rising from a chimney, flanked by two small outbuildings. The buildings were situated on a slight rise surrounded on three sides by trees. He was unable to see what lay on the far side of the cabin.

Hurrying as fast as he could, Clay made his way back to the cave and told Barbara what he had found. A cabin meant people, food, warmth, and maybe someone who could take them to the nearest town and—with luck—a doctor.

It took Barbara LaBonde almost an hour to work the sled close to the cabin. As they neared, Clay pointed out the fresh hide of a large bear hanging on a tree limb. He also noted that there was no more smoke rising from the chimney.

They knocked but got no response. Opening the unlocked door, they found no one inside, and though they were reluctant to enter uninvited, they were more reluctant to freeze to death. They stoked up the fire in the fireplace and sat close to warm themselves, waiting for the occupants to return.

Clay looked around the one-room cabin. Indicating the three cots with bedding on them, he quietly commented, "I sure hope the three hunters who are staying here are friendly."

Chapter Eleven

Safe from the elements in the hunters' cabin, Clay Edwards and Barbara LaBonde sat on ladder-back chairs in front of the fireplace. They were glad for the warmth of the cabin and certain that their horrible ordeal was over.

After a while Clay began to feel somewhat weak, remarking, "I think my walk this morning may have been too much, too soon."

"Not only that, but it's been a long time since you've had any nourishment at all," Barbara reminded him. Rising, she picked up the crude crutches and handed them to him. "Why don't you lie down over there on one of the cots?"

Smiling his agreement, Clay stood on his good leg and made his way across the spacious room to the front corner of the cabin. He sat on the cot and adjusted his gun belt, positioning the holster on the top of his thigh, then lay down.

Barbara came over and covered him with a blanket, looking down at him. Sighing, she said, "You need to eat, but I hate to touch the food and utensils that belong to whoever the occupants of this cabin are."

"You need some solid food yourself," Clay remarked. "Hunters are down-to-earth men and surely wouldn't mind sharing their food with two starving travelers."

She sighed again. "Perhaps you're right." Turning toward the kitchen area, the hardy brunette said, "Okay, I'll see what's here."

Barbara rummaged through the cupboard, finding that the hunters were quite well stocked with coffee, dried fruit, beans, corn meal, flour, lard, and other staples. "They must be on a long hunt," she told Clay. "They've got ample supplies. The only thing I can't find is any salted meat."

"Maybe they stay stocked up on fresh meat," suggested the ex-gunfighter. "Judging by that hide hanging outside, I'd guess they've got plenty of bear meat somewhere around here. Maybe it's in one of the sheds outside."

"I'll get a fire started in the stove, and then I'll go out and see," Barbara stated.

When the fire was going in the stove, she put on her coat and scarf, picked up a big butcher knife, and headed for the door. The cold air felt like a slap in the face as she stepped outside, and she pulled her coat more snugly around her.

Trudging through the snow, she headed around the cabin toward the sheds, one of which appeared to be used as a barn. The outbuildings were to one side and behind the cabin, and as she made her way to the one she felt might be used for meat storage, she noticed that some fifteen or so yards off to her left was the edge of a cliff. Assuming the vantage point would give her a view of the valley and possibly a town, she made her way to the lip and stopped short. The depth of the sheer drop was unexpected and dizzying, and she estimated that it was well over three hundred feet to the bottom of the canyon.

Returning to her mission, Barbara entered the smaller shed and found great slabs of fresh meat hanging from rafters on short lengths of rope. Using the butcher knife, she cut off a large hunk, finding that the meat was not yet frozen solid. Stepping out of the shed, meat in hand, she flicked a glance at the barn. Curious to learn what she could about the hunters, she hurried to the building and then slid the latch to look inside. She was surprised to find a generous supply of hay and several sacks of grain, and the amount of horse manure on the barn floor told her that animals had been there for some time.

Latching the shed, she hurried back to the cabin, looked toward Clay's cot, and smiled. "Found the bear meat," she announced. "I've got enough here to fill us both."

"Good," he replied, watching her as she walked to the counter.

She put down the meat and the knife, then removed her coat, meanwhile telling him about the cliff and what she found in the barn. "Judging by the stores here in the cabin and all the feed in the barn, the men occupying this place are planning to stay for some time," she concluded. "I don't think they're simply hunters. They live here."

"Maybe it's a family," suggested Clay. "You know, a man, his wife, and a son or daughter."

Barbara grinned, shaking her head. "No, Mr. Edwards. I can tell by the way this cabin looks that there are no women living here . . . just men."

"Oh. I guess a female would notice that kind of thing," Clay said. From his place on the cot he observed Barbara as she prepared the meal. Though the woolen dress she wore was high-necked and heavy, it did not hide her alluring figure. She would be desirable in the eyes of any red-blooded man—of which he was one. *Oh, Barbara,* he told her in his mind, *you have such a sweet spirit about you—except for your attitude toward men. Little lady, you are everything I have ever looked for in a woman. . . . bright, industrious, strong, spirited, and you've got grit.* He smiled to himself. Not to mention that she was the most beautiful woman he had ever seen. If he let himself, he knew he could fall in love with her.

The combined aroma of bear meat cooking and coffee heating made Clay salivate. Leaving the stove, Barbara crossed to the cot and told the injured man, "While the meat is cooking, I want to examine your leg."

Kneeling beside him, she unwrapped the makeshift bandage, laid aside the lengths of wood used as a splint, and pulled the leg of his pants up above his boot. Clay raised up on his elbows to look at the leg as Barbara chastised, "It's quite swollen—just as I thought it would be." She gave him a stern look. "You've got to stay off it as much as possible."

"Unless the occupants of this cabin have a wagon," he said, "I'll have to ride one of their horses to get to the nearest doctor. Since I'm not sure exactly where we are, I don't know how far that'll be." He gave her a wry grin. "Would you consider sitting in a saddle being off the leg?"

"No, I wouldn't," she replied sharply. "We'll have to ask one of the men to ride for the doctor and bring him here. Possibly the doctor can come in a wagon so he can take you back to his office for better care."

"Guess we really can't make any plans till those fellas show up, can we?" Clay mused.

"That's true," Barbara answered as she put the splints in place and began rewrapping them with the material.

While she carefully wound the cloth around the splints, Clay said softly, "You're very kind to take such good care of me. I want you to know that I appreciate it very much."

Barbara looked up from the knot she was tying. For a fleeting moment their eyes locked, and a smile tugged at the corners of her mouth. Clay felt a tingle run down his spine, and he was sure that Barbara was feeling something special toward him in return. Then, as if realizing that she had let her barrier down further than she'd intended, her expression abruptly hardened. She gave the cloth a jerk to finish the knot. Clay howled in pain.

Rising, she said flatly, "The food's going to burn," and hurried to the stove.

Repeatedly turning the sizzling meat in the skillet, Barbara purposely kept her back to the man on the cot across the room. When the meat was sufficiently browned, she added flour to the juices for gravy, and while she stirred it, she scolded herself for her feelings toward the tall, handsome ex-gunfighter. Steeling herself, she vowed that never again would she give her heart to a man—or ever trust one. Not one more time.

When the food was ready, Barbara said little to Clay

other than instructing him to sit at the table only long enough to eat and then to lie down again as soon as he had finished. During the meal, he periodically attempted to engage her in conversation, but she answered in monosyllables, and he soon gave up.

The wind picked up outside, and its howling was a mournful sound coming down the chimney. Barbara rose to add more logs to the fire, and Clay observed, "The wood supply is getting low. I'd venture that the occupants of this place are out cutting more." The brunette said nothing, and Clay hobbled back to the cot and lay down, again adjusting the holster and keeping the extra revolver beside his left leg.

He was surprised when Barbara crossed the room to cover him with the blanket and place pillows from the other cots under the broken leg, elevating it slightly. But her brusque manner prevented him from saying anything other than thank you, before she returned to the kitchen area to clean up. Sighing, Clay felt both frustrated and content. He closed his eyes and rested a forearm across his forehead, hoping he could find a way to penetrate Barbara's armor, but for the moment settling for the good feeling of food in his stomach and warmth in his bones.

Suddenly Barbara called, "Mr. Edwards . . ."

Clay lowered his arm and looked at her. She was staring through the window from the kitchen, straining to see out the frost-covered pane. "Yes?"

"Three riders just came into the yard, and one of them is a giant of a man. The two smaller men are riding double, and the third horse is pulling a sled full of cut wood."

"I guess I was right about the firewood—and we'll soon find out how welcome we are," Clay observed.

Still looking through the frosted glass, Barbara commented, "The bigger man has something wrong with his face, but with this frost, I can't quite make out what it is."

Outside, the three men pulled up and dismounted, gesturing at the crude sled left next to the porch, and noticing the smoke billowing from the chimney. Cursing, the huge man shouted, "Somebody's got a lot of gall! Just waltzed right through the door and moved in without an invite! Burnin' up our firewood, too! If he's touched our food . . ." He stomped toward the porch, saying over his shoulder to his companions, "Come on! Let's take care of him right now!"

The massive man flung the door open and halted in the doorway, stunned at the sight of the beautiful brunette who stood by the cupboard. As the man's companions drew up in back of him, the big man leered at Barbara and breathed, "Well, well. Where did you come from, honey? I was all set to throw the intruder out, but I sure ain't gonna throw *you* out! You can stay as long as you want— and as long as *I* want!"

Barbara stood like a statue.

One of the others crowded up closer and demanded, "Hey, let me'n Abe take a look at her!"

"*Look* is all you're gonna do, Eugene," warned the big man, moving inside. "Ain't nobody gonna touch her but me. I—" Just then Garth Candler spotted Clay Edwards lying on the cot in the corner. Glaring at the ex-gunfighter in disbelief, he roared, "You!"

Abe Willard and Eugene Hudson pushed inside behind their crony and stared at Clay. "Well, lookee who we got here!" Hudson snorted. "If it ain't our old pal the gunfighter!"

Candler took a step closer to Clay, who had not moved. The huge man's hatred was visible in his expression and demeanor. His yellow teeth bared, he pointed to the black patch covering his right eye and bellowed, "You blinded my eye, Edwards! If you hadn't been in solitary, I'd have killed you before I broke out of prison! I was gonna wait and kill you whenever you broke out, but I didn't know that day was comin' so soon!" Clawing for his gun, he hissed, "Appreciate your makin' it so easy for me!"

Barbara LaBonde reacted quickly. As Candler went

for his gun, she grabbed the heavy skillet from the stove and flung it at his head. It connected just above his right ear, knocking his hat from his bald head and throwing him off balance. At the same time, Willard and Hudson drew their guns to shoot the man on the cot.

But Clay had his revolvers ready under the blanket. He whipped them out and fired them before either of the outlaws could bring their weapons into play, and both men went down with bullets through their hearts.

While Clay was occupied in protecting himself, Candler once again moved to shoot the ex-gunfighter. Frantic, Barbara grabbed the butcher knife from the counter and leapt onto the giant's back, jabbing him in the side with the knife and then digging her fingers into his good eye.

Candler howled. He pulled the knife from his side and threw it to the floor, then spun around again and again, trying to dislodge the woman, but Barbara clung to the enormous man like a cocklebur, still clawing at his face. Clay was unable to get a clear shot at the convict without endangering Barbara, and when Candler staggered out the open door, the injured man struggled off the cot and limped to the brunette's rescue.

Stepping off the porch, the giant turned in a circle on the snow, trying to shake Barbara off. Clay followed, his weapon held at the ready, but when he saw it was useless to try to shoot, he holstered his gun and, forgetting his broken leg, ran after the huge outlaw. Suddenly Candler flipped Barbara over his head, slamming her to the snowy ground, and then felt his side. His fingers came away sticky and red with blood, and he stared at them as if disbelieving what he saw.

While the giant was distracted, Clay smashed into him, and the unexpected collision took Candler by surprise. He cursed loudly, and the horses began dancing around, frightened. The two men went down in the snow in a heap, flailing at one another. Pain lanced through Clay's leg, but he did his best to block it from his mind as he struggled to gain an advantage over the giant. Somehow he had to snuff out Candler's life, for if he did not, Candler would kill him—and if that happened, a fate worse than death awaited Barbara LaBonde.

Lying in the snow, her hair in disarray and hanging in her face, Barbara gasped for breath, unable to move. For several seconds the two adversaries threshed wildly just a few feet from her, but then they rolled over several times, staining the snow with Candler's blood and thrusting themselves farther from the house.

Candler's size and weight made it impossible for Clay to wrestle him into submission. He knew his only chance was to stun the giant with his fists. If he could get free of Candler's clutches and daze him with a couple of hard punches, he knew he could pull his gun and the fight would be over.

After a few moments Clay was able to slam an elbow into Candler's nose hard enough to slow him. Immediately, he stood, favoring his bad leg, and as the huge man scrambled to his feet, Clay caught him on the jaw with a solid blow. He felt the pain shoot all the way from his fist to his shoulder, but it toppled the bigger man. Limping back a couple of steps, Clay grabbed for his gun.

It was gone.

His heart leapt to his throat as he looked around in the snow to find the revolver, aware that the giant was getting up. The weapon was nowhere to be seen.

Shaking his head and rubbing at the eye Barbara had scratched, Garth snarled, "I'm gonna tear you into little pieces, Edwards!"

The giant lumbered toward him, fists swinging. Backtracking, the ex-gunfighter suddenly found himself up against a tree. As a big, meaty fist shot at his face, Clay ducked, the bones in Candler's hand cracking when fist met trunk.

The pain distracted Candler for a moment, and Clay was able to land a few solid blows to the bigger man's face and nose. Candler staggered, shaking his head. Then, remembering that he had a gun in his holster, he clawed for it. Clay, seeing this, grabbed the wrist of Candler's gun hand, and they struggled around in a circle until the smaller man slammed the giant's hand against a tree. The weapon discharged and the slug chewed into the shed by the skittish horses. The terrified animals bolted, heading into the woods. The horse hitched to the sled followed the others, the sled fishtailing wildly for a short distance until it hit a pine tree and smashed; then the horse galloped away with the broken harness flying behind it.

Barbara LaBonde finally groped to her knees, trying to stand and desperately looking around for a weapon of some kind. With the aid of a tree, she managed to get to her feet, determined to help Clay finish off the killer. Letting go of the tree, she turned to head for the cabin when she spotted the revolver lying in the snow. She picked it up, brushed the snow from it, and slowly started toward the combatants.

Before Garth Candler could cock his gun again, Clay Edwards slammed the man's hand against the tree a second time. The weapon flew out of Candler's hand, disappearing into a deep snowbank. Wheeling, Candler made a dive for the gun, tearing at the snow, but Clay leapt onto his back and grabbed his thick neck to keep him from getting his hands on the revolver.

They grappled in the snow, getting farther from the house and closer to the edge of the cliff. Releasing Candler's neck, Clay scrambled to his feet and pain shot through his leg. He felt a wave of nausea wash over him and saw spots in front of his eyes. *No!* he screamed to himself. *Don't pass out now!*

Aware that his adversary was in trouble, Candler smirked and planted his feet in the snow. Wiping blood from his nose, he growled, "Now you die, little man!"

Before Clay could maneuver himself away from the killer's grasp, Candler scooped him up and tossed him over his shoulder, carrying him toward the cliff.

"Stop or I'll shoot!" Barbara shouted from far behind. But the killer laughed and kept walking. "No, you won't," he shouted back. "You'd be afraid of hittin' your boyfriend."

Clay glimpsed the precipice as the giant carried him. Twisting and writhing to free himself as they neared it, he saw blood oozing from Candler's right side. Doubling up his fist, he pounded the huge man square on his wound.

Candler gasped and faltered. Clay hit him again, and the giant's legs buckled. Three more hard blows dropped Candler to his knees, gasping, and Clay rolled free. The rim of the canyon was ten feet away, and a bone-chilling wind whistled up out of its depths. He glanced back and saw Barbara trudging toward him, but the snow was well over two feet deep in the open area, making it slow going for her.

Desperate to end the ordeal, Clay grabbed Candler's feet and, grunting with effort, dragged his huge adversary toward the edge of the cliff. Candler clawed at the snow, trying to stop Clay's progress. Just as Clay prepared to roll him into the canyon, Candler managed to twist away. Jerking his legs loose, he kicked Clay's broken leg.

Clay screamed in agony but willed his head to stay clear. He staggered dangerously close to the icy edge, but moved away as Candler got to his feet. Summoning every ounce of strength he could muster, Clay sent a violent blow to the giant's wound. Candler bellowed in pain and staggered, but he countered with a fist of his own. As he swung, his back was to the yawning chasm and he was slightly off balance. Clay saw his opportunity.

Standing as securely as possible, he smashed the huge man's chin with a savage punch. Candler reeled backward, and a shocked, despairing cry tore from his throat as he plummeted into the snowy depths below.

Exhausted, panting for air, Clay turned around to see Barbara standing knee-deep in the snow thirty feet behind him, holding his revolver. He expected to see relief on her face, but instead there was fire in her eyes. Puzzled, he limped toward her, dragging his broken leg. The pain was almost unbearable, and as he struggled through the snow, he gasped, "It's all right now . . . Mrs. LaBonde. All . . . of them . . . are dead."

Cold though it was, the brunette's face was flushed. Glaring at Clay, she shouted, "Why didn't you tell me that you're a convict—an escaped convict, at that?"

Drawing close, he admitted, "Well . . . technically I'm a convict, yes. But you see—"

"And to think I was beginning to trust you!" she burst out. "I thought I had finally met a man I could trust!"

His eyes begged for understanding. "You can!" he insisted.

"Hah!" she countered scornfully. "You said you're an ex-gunfighter who has taken up ranching—but in fact you're a criminal! An escaped convict! You . . . you—"

Before the furious woman could find the right word to call him, Clay suddenly turned white and collapsed, unconscious. Sighing, Barbara knelt beside him. She rammed the revolver into Clay's holster, then pulled him back to the cabin.

Barbara managed to get him onto the cot and remove the splints to examine his leg. Finding that it needed resetting, she was glad—despite her anger—that Clay was still unconscious and would not feel further pain.

With his leg reset and rebandaged, the spunky woman set about removing the other outlaws' bodies from the cabin. After removing their gun belts and leaving them on a shelf near the door, she hauled the corpses to the edge of the cliff one at a time and rolled them into the canyon to join Garth Candler. Then she made herself a pot of coffee and waited for Clay Edwards to come to—and tell her the truth.

Chapter Twelve

Clay Edwards slowly regained consciousness, aware first of the pain in his leg and then of sounds coming from nearby. Running his tongue over parched lips, he opened his eyes to see Barbara LaBonde stacking logs next to the fireplace. When she had finished, she dusted off her gloves and then headed toward the door, where she took off her coat and scarf and hung them on a wall peg. On a shelf over the peg were a couple of gun belts, and Clay immediately looked to where Candler's cronies had fallen from his bullets. Their bodies were gone.

Barbara then returned to the fireplace and picked up the iron poker to flip a couple of blazing logs over. Leaning the poker against the stone front of the fireplace, she stood back to watch the flames.

As she turned and started walking toward Clay, he recalled everything that had taken place just prior to his passing out. He noticed that she was wearing a different dress. She had obviously changed into dry clothes while he had been passed out. He also noticed that she had brushed her hair, which curled down over her shoulders in a way he found most attractive.

There was no smile either on her lips or in her eyes as she stood over him and asked tersely, "Leg hurting?"

"Like fury," he replied.

"I had to set it again."

"I appreciate all you've done. Thank you."

"You're welcome," she said flatly, obviously still net-
tled. The wind gave off a haunting moan as it blew around
the eaves of the cabin outside, and it seemed to mirror the
look in her eyes. "Anything I can get you?" she asked.

"I could use some water. My mouth's awfully dry."

Nodding, Barbara went to the counter and dipped a
tin cup in the water bucket. She came back and wordlessly
handed him the cup. He could almost feel the angry hurt
in her eyes as he drained the water. Handing the cup
back, he thanked her, smiling weakly.

She started to turn away, but halted as he said, "Please,
I'd like to explain things to you."

Barbara hung the handle of the tin cup on a thumb,
folded her arms, and asked sarcastically, "You're not going
to give me the same old story that I'm sure ninety percent
of the convicts in that place spin, are you? The 'I'm
innocent' routine? I lived in Canon City, Mr. Edwards,
and I knew some of the guards. I also know all about what
they hear from prisoners."

Looking Barbara straight in the eye, Clay said, "You've
been around me for a few days now. Do *you* think I'm a
criminal? Do I behave like a man who walks on the other
side of the law?"

Barbara's face tinted slightly. "No," she admitted softly.

"Do you believe in the letter of the law, Mrs.
LaBonde?"

"Certainly."

"Isn't it true in a democracy that a person stands
innocent until proven guilty?"

"Yes—and you must've been proven guilty in a court
of law or you would not have been sent to prison."

"I was framed, ma'am," Clay responded. "By an outlaw named C.K. Moxley, who has a hideout near Buckskin
Pass. The only way I can prove my innocence is to force
him to tell the truth to the law, and there wasn't any way I
could do that while sitting behind bars in the state penitentiary. I broke out so I could find Moxley and clear

myself. That's the truth, and it sure would mean a lot to me if you'd let me tell you what happened."

"All right," Barbara said with a sigh, dropping her arms and sitting on the cot beside Clay, "I'll listen."

The ex-gunfighter related every detail of his story, from the day of the bank robbery in Gunnison till he met the stagecoach, including what he had done to Nick Framm after escaping and the reason there was animosity between himself and Garth Candler. He finished by saying, "I realize all you have at this point is my word on this, but would you let me stand innocent in your eyes until I can prove it? Once I'm cleared, I'll come to your sister's house and give you written evidence."

Barbara looked at him askance. "Why is it so important to you how I feel?"

Clay looked into her eyes for a long moment. He could not bring himself to say what was really on his mind, and instead replied, "We've been through a lot together these past several days. I'd like to believe that we've become friends. It just means a lot to me, what you think of me."

Barbara's face softened, and her eyes lost their pained look. "I'm sorry, Mr. Edwards. You certainly aren't a criminal. Twice you saved my life at the risk of your own. Those terrible men stretched my nerves pretty tight, and when I heard them say you were in prison with them, it was just more than I could handle. Please forgive me. I believe your story . . . every word of it. You don't have to prove a thing to me."

A smile lit up Clay Edward's face. "Thank you, ma'am." He sighed. "I feel a whole lot better now."

Clay's smile was contagious, and Barbara smiled in return.

Tilting his head, Clay asked, "*Are* we friends, Mrs. LaBonde?"

"Yes," she replied vigorously, her smile widening. "We are friends."

"Good!" he said, shifting on the cot. "Then could we

be less formal than Mr. Edwards and Mrs. LaBonde? May I call you Barbara?"

Chuckling, the brunette answered, "Yes, you can call me Barbara . . . Clay."

"Ah, that's a whole lot better," he declared, laughing.

Noticing that his pillow was slipping, Barbara leaned over him, saying, "Here, let me adjust this before it falls."

As she repositioned the pillow, their eyes met and held. The magnetic warmth in Clay's dark brown eyes seemed to attract Barbara's head toward his. Their lips were only inches apart when she suddenly pulled away and stood up, her heart pounding.

Looking down at him, the young woman murmured, "I'm sorry. Forgive me for having a weak moment."

Clay swallowed hard. "There's nothing to forgive, Barbara. Something's happening between us. Don't fight it. Let's just—"

"No!" she snapped. Then moderating her voice, she said, "I have to be honest with you. Too much has happened in my life. I've told you before that I just can't trust another man again, and I mean it."

Clay sat up and gazed intently into her eyes. "Barbara, I must be honest with *you*. I'm falling in love with you."

The beautiful brunette looked at him for a moment, unspeaking. Then, standing up straight, she changed the subject by saying, "You told me of your purpose in wanting to go to Buckskin Pass, but it seems to me you're in for a long wait. You can't go up against this Moxley until your leg is healed—and besides, he no doubt has a whole gang around him."

Clay's countenance changed. The hatred he held for Moxley showed in his eyes as he said raggedly, "I can handle it. I'm going after him as soon as I can get there. That dirty rat is going to clear me if I have to torture him to make him do it."

Barbara had been about to comment when her eye

caught movement outside through the back window. She rushed over and Clay called after her, "What's the matter?"

"I saw something move out back," she replied, not taking her gaze from the window. Using the warmth of her palm to thaw the thin layer of frost from the center of the pane, Barbara looked back and forth, studying the area in view for a long moment.

Clay sat up on the cot, throwing the blanket off. "See anything?"

"No."

"What do you think you saw?"

Still looking through the window, Barbara wiped her hand over it again. "I'm not sure," she replied. "With the window frosted up, I couldn't see anything clearly, but I'm sure I saw a dark form move past the window."

Picking up his tree-limb crutches off the floor, Clay stood, leaning on them. As he hobbled toward her he said, "Are you thinking that perhaps it was an Indian?"

Turning to look at him, her face was pale. "Yes. That's exactly what I'm thinking."

Clay drew up beside her and peered through the window. "I seriously doubt it's Indians," he said reassuringly. "You wouldn't have seen them unless they wanted you to—and they'd have just come busting through the door before we knew they were here. They wouldn't pass by a window and take the chance of being seen and give us opportunity to arm ourselves. Besides, they—"

Just then a big bull moose came into view, nosing around from the side of the building. Chuckling, Clay announced, "There's your Indian."

Her hand went to the base of her throat and she let out a sigh of relief. "Oh," she said, hearing her pulse pounding in her ears. "I feel so foolish."

Laughing and relaxed, Clay and Barbara were just turning from the window when the front door of the cabin burst open, slamming against the wall. Barbara jumped with fright and let out a shriek. A shiver of fear rippled up her spine and, her eyes huge, she moved close to Clay, who stood as if stunned. Framed in the doorway, back from the dead, was Garth Candler.

Battered, bloody, and insane with rage, Candler glared at the couple. In his hand was the snow-packed revolver he had lost in the fight, having obviously found it while making his way back to the cabin. Patches of snow were caked to his clothing, and he was leaning toward the right, favoring his wounded side, which was still oozing blood.

Breathing heavily, the massive man snarled, "You didn't hit me hard enough, Edwards! Instead of goin' to the bottom of the canyon, I landed on a ledge. That'll prove to be a fatal mistake"—he flicked his malevolant stare at Barbara—"for both of you!"

Feeling helpless, Clay eyed his guns across the room on the cot. Willard's and Hudson's revolvers were also out of reach, and he did not know where Barbara had put the Winchesters that had been on the sled.

Before Clay could make any kind of a move, Candler raised the gun in his hand, cocked the hammer, then aimed it point-blank at Clay's chest and squeezed the trigger. But the icy snow that packed the barrel prevented the firing pin from striking. Furious, the giant looked disbelievingly at the gun, shook it, and hurriedly attempted to thumb the hammer back again.

Moving swiftly, Clay used one of his crutches as a club and hurled it violently at Candler. It struck him in the face, knocking him into the frame of the open door. While Clay hobbled as quickly as he could toward the revolvers on the shelf, the killer threw his useless gun at his enemy. But the weapon merely whistled past Clay's head and hit the back wall. Roaring like a frenzied grizzly, Candler charged.

Startled to her senses, Barbara swung into action. Before the two men collided, Barbara seized the fireplace poker and darted toward the giant.

Though Candler was hindered by his wound and the battering he had taken in the fall, his hundred-pound advantage was enough to knock the smaller Edwards off his feet when they connected. But as Clay went down, Barbara rushed in, swinging the deadly poker in a wide arc and aiming for the big bald head. Candler saw it coming and dodged it, then whacked her flush on the jaw with a huge fist, knocking her across the room. She slammed against the back wall and lay dazed.

Clay was on his feet again, dragging his splinted leg as he beelined for the shelf. Candler pivoted, saw where he was headed, and lunged for him. They fell to the floor, rolling and fighting wildly, ending up at the fireplace.

The killer attempted to push Clay into the fire, shoving the ex-gunfighter's head onto the edge of the hearth. Clay felt the sudden surge of heat and fought back with all his might. As he was pushed ever closer to the licking flames, Clay's flailing hand found the wood stack and he gripped a log. He brought it savagely against the side of Candler's head, stunning him momentarily and dislodging the black eyepatch, exposing an empty socket where the eyeball had been.

Clay wriggled free and began crawling toward the shelf and the two revolvers. He was halfway across the room and, using a chair for support, got to his feet. Dragging the bad leg, he pressed toward his goal, but Candler suddenly bounded after him, his mouth gaping and his expression wild. Just as Clay was within reach of the shelf, the giant caught him and spun him around. They grappled for a moment, then Candler hit him solidly. Clay went reeling from the impact of the blow and landed beside his cot.

Laughing fiendishly, Candler reached to the shelf and pulled one of the guns from its holster. He whirled around, anticipation written on his face, but then checked his motion. Clay Edwards was sitting on the floor with both his revolvers cocked and aimed at the killer's chest. Gasping for breath, Clay snapped, "Drop the gun or you're a dead man!"

The massive man had not yet cocked or aimed the revolver, but he clearly was beyond thinking reasonably.

Without hesitation he thumbed the hammer back and brought the weapon to bear.

Clay fired his right-hand gun, hitting Candler in the chest. The loud, sharp sound reverberated off the cabin's four walls as Candler slammed against the wall behind him. He faltered for an instant but then regained his balance and brought the gun up again.

Clay fired the other gun. The bullet tore into Candler's right shoulder. His arm jumped up and he reflexively let go of the gun. It flew from his hand and clattered across the floor, out of reach. Spotting the fireplace poker, he grabbed for it and turned to face his foe.

Holding both guns ready to fire, Clay warned, "Don't try it, Candler!"

Ignoring the warning, the big man stormed toward Clay like a cornered, wounded beast. Both of Clay's revolvers roared, hitting Candler point-blank. Stumbling, the big man dropped the poker on the floor. A rattling sound came from his throat as he took one last step and then toppled like a felled tree, collapsing on top of Clay, the bulk of his weight landing violently on Clay's broken leg.

Screaming with pain, Clay was barely aware of Barbara standing and moving toward him. Then he passed out.

When Clay Edwards came to, he was lying on the floor, a pillow under his head, and Barbara LaBonde was seated in a chair beside him. It took several moments for his vision to fully clear, but when it finally did, he looked up at her and asked, "Are you all right?"

"I've got a pretty sore jaw," she answered, smiling slightly, "but other than that, I'm fine."

"Candler . . ."

"You killed him with those last two shots. Sorry I couldn't get you back onto the cot, but I ran out of strength after hauling his body out of here and shoving it over the cliff." She smiled grimly. "This time he went all the way to the bottom—joining his pals."

"My leg . . . I remember—"

"I set it again," she cut in, "but I want to get you to a doctor as soon as possible. It's in pretty bad shape, having been repeatedly reinjured, and there's no way for me to know if I've set it properly. I've got the sled loaded and ready to go, but I think we should wait until morning to head out." She gave him another weak smile. "After everything that's happened today, I'm exhausted. I wouldn't have the strength to pull an *empty* sled. Besides, it'll be better that you rest for a night, too. It's almost evening, so I'll fix us a good supper, and then we'll get a good night's rest. We'll both feel more like traveling in the morning."

When they set out the next morning, the sky was leaden and a storm was brewing. Determined to get Clay Edwards the help he needed, Barbara LaBonde pressed into the rope and pulled the sled behind her, heading north. The wind blew ceaselessly straight into her face, and by the time they had traveled an hour, the snow was coming down hard.

From his place on the sled Clay called, "Maybe we'd better turn back!"

The resolute woman paused and shouted above the howling wind, "Clay, if I haven't set your leg properly and it begins to heal that way, you'll limp for the rest of your life! We've got to keep going! I must find a ranch so someone can help me get you to a doctor!"

Complying with her determination, Clay let her tug the sled for nearly another hour, until the storm turned into a wild blizzard. Defeated by the elements, Barbara shouted, "I'm sorry, Clay! We'd better return to the cabin before we get lost out here!"

Four hours after they had left the cabin, Clay and Barbara were back within its sheltering walls with a fire roaring. The blizzard lasted for three days. On the morning of the fourth day, when the sun finally shone again,

Barbara took one look out a frosty window at the enormous snowdrifts surrounding the house. Her heart sank.

Turning to her companion, she said dully, "We might as well face it. You and I are stuck here for the winter."

"I'd say you're right," Clay responded. "But I don't want you worrying about my leg. I'm sure you did a fine job setting it."

Sighing, she moved to the cot beside his and sat down. "There are axes and a saw in the shed where the bear meat is hanging. We'll have to cut plenty of wood to make it, but at least we don't have to worry about food, and I'll do my best to take care of your leg." She paused, then said, "I want to lay down the law to you, Clay. You've declared your feelings for me, but you must forget them. I'm never going to give my heart to another man, and you must not make any romantic moves toward me. Is it agreed?"

With reluctance, the rugged ex-gunfighter ran his fingers through his curly hair and said softly, "If you insist."

Praying that C. K. Moxley would still be at Buckskin Pass when the thaw came, Clay Edwards settled in with Barbara LaBonde to wait for spring.

Chapter Thirteen

It was early April when the spring thaw came. Clay Edwards's leg had healed, but it was evident that he would walk with a slight limp for the rest of his life. Not at all discouraged, he and Barbara LaBonde decided to head north toward Buena Vista, where they hoped to obtain horses. Eager to get to Buckskin Pass as soon as possible, and hoping that C. K. Moxley had not left his hideout, they planned to leave the following morning, April 10, 1885.

Clay slid into his mackinaw after breakfast, donned his Stetson, and told Barbara, "I'm going out to hunt us down a few squirrels to take along when we head out tomorrow. Since we're not quite sure where we are, I want to make sure we have enough meat to tide us over until we run into a ranch or town." He grinned, adding, "While that bear was mighty big, there isn't much left of him."

Pausing in her dish washing, Barbara smiled at the handsome man, nodded her agreement, then watched him pick up one of the Winchester repeaters and step outside. When the door had closed behind him, she ran across the room to one of the front windows and peered out, watching him trudge through the snow that was still about a foot deep. When he had passed from view, she slowly headed back toward the counter, wringing her hands.

Passing the mirror that hung on the cabin's back wall,

she stopped and looked at it, thinking of the many times she had watched Clay shave himself in front of it over the past several months. *Just one more time,* she reminded herself, *and then we'll be gone from this place.*

Barbara regarded her reflection in the glass. Tears suddenly filled her eyes and spilled down her cheeks. "What are you going to do, Barbara?" she asked herself aloud. "Once you and Clay get horses, it won't take long to reach Apsen. He'll leave you there and ride out of your life forever."

Suddenly overwhelmed by the prospect of never seeing Clay again, Barbara turned away from the mirror and sat down at the table, sobbing. Finally wiping her face on her dish towel, she thought about the winter she and Clay had shared.

Though he had looked upon her lovingly every day, he had respected her wishes and made no move toward her. They had whiled away the many long hours talking, and she had enjoyed his company immensely. Now that they were about to leave the cabin, she was having serious problems with her feelings. By the last week of January, Barbara knew she had fallen in love with Clay Edwards. His kindness, good looks, rugged masculinity, and charming, tender ways had won her over. For months she had kept up a crusty façade, trying to keep Clay from knowing she had fallen in love with him, but now that they were about to leave, the thought of never seeing him again was tearing her apart.

Clenching her fists, she rested her head against them and wept softly, reminding herself that she'd vowed never to give her heart to another man. The scars left by Jack would be a thousand times deeper the next time. She couldn't go through that kind of pain again!

She thought of how Clay had talked all winter about wanting to get back to ranching once he cleared himself, hoping one day to have his own spread. But because she had stubbornly insisted on keeping a wall between them, he had said nothing about wanting her to share the future with him. Nevertheless she had seen his longing for her in his eyes. *If only she had let him express it!*

Tortured by her ambivalence, she was also fearful that Clay would be killed in his attempt to squeeze the truth from C. K. Moxley. She shook her head, forcing the horrible thought from her mind.

Drying her tears, Barbara finished her chores before Clay returned. Then, glancing out the window where she had last seen the ex-gunfighter, terror suddenly knifed through her heart. Five Ute braves were dismounting from their pintos at the front porch!

Barbara's heart beat wildly as she ran across the room and bolted the door. As she picked up a revolver from the shelf, the Indians began battering the door, trying to break it down. Trembling, she squared herself with the door and fired the gun straight into it. There was a scream and the pounding momentarily stopped, but then it started again. A tiny whimper rose from her throat as she fired repeatedly through the door. When the hammer clicked down on an empty chamber, Barbara dashed to the shelf for the other revolver.

Suddenly the door crashed open and four wild-eyed Utes plunged inside. Before the young woman could grab another gun, the warriors seized her and dragged her outside. As they forced her through the doorway, she trod on the outstretched hand of the fifth Indian, lying dead on the porch.

Fighting with every ounce of strength in her body, Barbara kicked, twisted, and screamed as the Indians hoisted her onto the back of the leader's pinto. He quickly swung up behind her, holding her while the others picked up the dead Indian and draped him over the back of one of the other horses. The Utes goaded their ponies and headed eastward, in the same direction Clay had gone. Barbara screamed at the top of her lungs, praying the sound would carry to him.

The ex-gunfighter was slogging through the snow with several dead squirrels strung on a thin rope, heading back to the cabin. He had been standing beside a swift-moving stream swollen by melting snow when Barbara fired the six shots, and he had not heard them. As he walked back through the heavy timber, he thought he heard something ahead of him, and he stopped so he could listen without the crunching of snow interfering. It came again . . . a woman's scream. *Barbara!*

The breath froze in Clay's throat and a shiver ran up his spine. Dropping the squirrels, he broke into a run, bounding through the snow and threading his way among the trees. The scream was repeated, and Clay could tell that it was getting closer.

Suddenly he caught a glimpse of riders crossing a small clearing about a hundred yards ahead. Utes! They were coming straight toward him, and the one in the lead had Barbara on his horse.

Thinking fast, Clay leapt behind a snow-laden boulder and ducked down, jacking a cartridge into the chamber of his rifle. He then removed his hat and rose up enough to keep the Indians in sight. Planning his move, he decided he would cut down the three braves who trailed and then grab a pinto to go after the one who had Barbara. Since the lead horse had a double load, Clay figured he would soon be able to catch up to it.

Clapping his hat back on his head, he hunkered down behind the boulder and waited. Barbara was still screaming. Moments later the fast-moving procession passed him, and he rose and shot the last Ute in line off his horse. The pinto that he led galloped away, spilling the corpse from its back.

Hearing the shot, the rest of the Indians pulled rein. The leader looked over his shoulder, shouting something in Ute as Clay shot another man, sending him into the snow. Working the lever, he aimed and blasted the third one into eternity. Barbara called his name as the leader goaded his animal and took off at a fast clip.

Grabbing the Winchester, Clay dashed to one of the pintos that had not run off, grabbed the reins, and swung onto its back. Snow flew behind the horse and rider as the determined man put the pinto into as fast a gait as the animal could muster.

The Ute leader guided his pinto through the thick timber and then swung out into a broad meadow carpeted with snow. Looking behind him, he pushed the pinto hard until his pursuer reached the meadow, and then he halted and swung up his rifle. He had shouldered the weapon to draw a bead on Clay when Barbara shoved it hard, spoiling his aim.

The unobstructed sunshine in the meadow had melted the snow several inches below that in the forest, and Clay was coming on fast. Dropping his single-shot rifle, the Ute locked Barbara in his arm and put his mount into a gallop.

Clay was unable to get a clear shot at the Indian for fear of hitting Barbara, and the race went on for several minutes, but he soon found he had been right. The double load on the Indian's horse was slowing it down, giving Clay the advantage, and within the next hundred yards he gained ground and pulled alongside the Ute.

Barbara suddenly elbowed the warrior hard in the stomach, and he released her in surprise. It was just the opportunity Clay needed. Dropping his rifle, he sprang from his horse onto the Ute, and the two men then sailed off the animal and plowed into the snow.

Grabbing the reins, Barbara soon brought the pinto to a halt. She whirled it around and trotted it back toward the two combatants, who were now standing. The Ute had his knife in hand, wielding it in wide arcs at Clay's belly, clearly wanting to slice his enemy open. But the agile white man managed to avoid the deadly blade.

As the men circled one another, Clay, taller and more muscular, faced the fierce-looking Ute with grim determination. Knees bent in readiness and arms spread wide for quick action, he dodged the knife repeatedly as the Indian came at him with murder in his dark eyes. Clay caught a glimpse of Barbara as she slid from the pinto's back and began searching for his rifle in the snow and tall grass.

Eager to kill the white man, the Indian abruptly lunged for Clay, attempting to plunge the knife straight into his chest. But his foe grabbed his arm, twisted it around, and flipped him over his back. The warrior hit the snow, but quickly got to his feet and came at Clay again, still wielding the deadly weapon. Once more he swung it in a wide arc, attempting to cut through the mackinaw and lay open the white man's midsection; however, Clay crouched low and the knife, glinting in the sunlight, slashed harmlessly over his head.

Scooping up a handful of snow, Clay threw it in the Ute's face. The tiny ice crystals mixed in with the snow stung the Indian's eyes, and he staggered for a moment, blinking. Clay sprang at him like a panther and grabbed the knife arm with both hands. Raising his knee, he brought the arm down on it so violently that the bone cracked. The Ute screamed in pain and dropped the knife into the snow.

The ex-gunfighter then smashed the Indian in the jaw with his fist and felled him. The Ute struggled to get up, but his bigger opponent sent another powerful blow to his temple, and the Indian went down, shaking his head. Grunting, he got to his knees, clearly ready to continue the fight with the hated white man, but his enemy was nowhere in sight. The Indian was looking left and right when a pair of powerful arms seized him from behind.

Barbara called to Clay, saying she had found his rifle, but her words came too late. Clay had already clamped the Indian's head in the crook of his arm from behind, and with the other hand he gripped the warrior's chin. Giving the head a violent, abrupt twist, he cracked the man's spine. The Ute went limp in Clay's grasp.

Breathing heavily, Clay dropped the dead Indian and looked at Barbara. Her eyes were bulging from what she had just beheld. Gasping between breaths, Clay asked, "Are you . . . all right?"

Licking her lips, the wide-eyed woman nodded. "Y-Yes."

"What . . . happened?

Barbara described the Indians' arrival at the cabin and her killing one before they broke in and captured her.

Smiling, Clay said, "Ah, so that's why they had a dead one with them."

Barbara handed Clay his Winchester. As he hefted it he said, "We've got to ditch the bodies of these Indians in case some of their pals come looking for them anytime soon." He grinned. "At least we got us a couple of horses out of this ordeal."

She laughed. "That's one of the things I like best about you, Clay. You always find the positive side of things."

Working fast, they dumped the bodies of the Utes in a deep crevice at the edge of the forest. They then rode quickly back to the cabin, hurriedly packed their belongings into a couple of gunny sacks, then mounted up, each carrying one of the Winchesters. They wanted to get as far from the area as possible before any more Utes showed up.

Heading steadily north, it took them nearly an hour to find the road they had been traveling on so long ago. The warmth of the sun was slowly melting the snow on the road, and little rivulets of water trickled along its sides. Glad to have their bearings at last and be on their way toward Aspen, they stopped to let the horses rest at the top of a long incline. Clay did not relax his vigil, however. He squinted against the glare off the sea of white that surrounded them, checking their back trail for any sign of Indians.

Barbara was beside him, astride her pinto, and she remarked, "If we're caught by the Utes with these horses, there's no telling what they'll do to us."

"They'd kill us," he replied, studying the area to the south. "But the worst part would be what they would do to us *before* they allowed us to die. We're just going to have to keep moving at a good pace, so—"

Abruptly, he stopped speaking. He'd spotted movement in a valley some distance south. Barbara looked at him, then shot a glance in the direction he was looking. "Do you see them?" she queried with a trembling voice.

"I'm not sure," he answered, peering intently into the valley. "There was movement, but . . . There!" he exclaimed, pointing. "Do you see it?"

Using her hand to shade her eyes against the brilliant sunlight, Barbara searched the vista. "I don't see anything."

Still pointing directly south, Clay asked, "See that small frozen pond just this side of that large patch of trees?"

"Yes."

"Now look right between the pond and the edge of the trees. There's a lone rider making straight toward us."

"Now I see," she said, nodding. "He seems to be on a solid-colored dark horse, and he's dressed in dark clothing." She looked at Clay and was visibly more relaxed. "He's not an Indian, that's for sure. I'd say we've nothing to worry about from him."

"Not for you, maybe, but he could mean trouble for me. Remember that guy I told you about? Nick Framm?"

"Yeah."

"It could be him. He swore he'd break out and come after me. Or"—a cold chill coursed through Clay's body—"it could be a federal marshal looking for me now that winter's over. I hope it's neither, but it's safer if I assume the man is on my trail. Let's ride." Pushing the pintos hard, they galloped northward.

During the next two days, Clay Edwards and Barbara LaBonde passed through Buena Vista and a couple of smaller towns. Periodically they caught glimpses of the lone rider in the distance behind them, and with every sighting Clay became more certain that the man was on his trail.

At midmorning on the third day they rode into Aspen under a clear sky. Barbara guided Clay through the town and then led him off the main thoroughfare onto a side street, drawing up in front of a small log cabin. As she slid from the pinto's back, advising Clay that this was her sister's house, Barbara's heart was aching. The moment she had dreaded was now upon her.

Clay's feet had just touched the ground when the door of the cabin flew open and a young woman who strongly resembled Barbara in size, features, and hair color came darting out. While the sisters embraced, Clay decided that though Susan and Barbara looked a great deal alike, Barbara was the more beautiful.

Taking her older sibling by the hand, Barbara led her to the tall, handsome ex-gunfighter and said, "Clay, I want you to meet my sister. Susan, this is Clay Edwards."

Susan Granville greeted Clay cordially, and then Barbara took three or four minutes to give her sister a brief explanation of what had transpired in the past several months, including Clay's being framed and sent to prison, his escape, the death of Jack LaBonde, and Clay's purpose in wanting to get to Buckskin Pass.

Susan declared, "My goodness! I'm grateful that you never had the opportunity to wire me and tell me you were coming! When the stagecoach never arrived, it was presumed that the crew and passengers were dead somewhere along the way—and I would have thought that you were among them." Thanking Clay for saving her sister's life, Susan then asked, "Do you know how to get to the pass, Mr. Edwards?"

"I know it's about ten miles due west of here," he replied.

"That's right. It's a little farther northwest of Maroon Bells Peaks, and they're easy to spot. Maroon Lake is just south of it. You can't miss the trail. The pass tops out at nearly twelve thousand feet. Do you know on which side of the pass your Mr. Moxley has his hideout?"

"No, ma'am, but I'll find it. Thanks for the directions." Clay then turned to Barbara and said, "I must get going. If that man trailing us is a federal marshal, he'll want to stop me from getting to Moxley—and I'll never be cleared if that happens."

Barbara felt a tremor run through her body and her throat went tight. She was certain that if she tried to speak, nothing would come out.

Clay touched his hat brim and said to Susan, "Nice to have met you, ma'am." He then looked deep into Barbara's eyes, saying softly, "Well, little lady, I guess this is good-bye. Thanks for the sled ride. I wouldn't have made it without you."

Fighting against the constriction in her throat, Barbara took hold of Clay's hands and murmured, "I'll want to know how it turns out. Will you stop back here when it's over?"

A shadow seemed to fall across Clay Edwards's face. Clearly suppressing his pain, his mouth was a thin line as he replied soberly, "It'll be better if I just write you, Barbara. You see, I . . . I'm in love with you now more than ever, but since you don't feel the same way about me, there's no sense in our seeing each other again. I will never forget you, and I will always love you, but it's better that we say good-bye right now."

Taking his hands from hers, Clay gripped the beautiful woman's shoulders and kissed her tenderly on the cheek. Then he rushhed to his horse. Tears coursed down her cheeks as Barbara LaBonde watched Clay Edwards mount the pinto and head the horse due west. He rode away without looking back.

A sudden surge of anguish gripped the young woman's heart, and her hands trembled as she put them to her cheeks. In her mind one voice cried for her to call Clay back and confess her love for him. The other voice warned sharply that he would only hurt her as Jack did. The first voice lashed back, *You're not being fair to Clay! He has declared his love for you, and he should not be judged on the basis of what Jack did . . . or what your father and brothers did, for that matter!*

Barbara felt her sister's hands on her shoulders. "Are you in love with him, Barbie?"

The brunette nodded and replied with a shaky voice, "Most desperately."

"Then don't let him ride out of your life! Call him back! Give yourself a chance at some happiness. The Lord knows you deserve it!"

The wall Barbara LaBonde had built up suddenly crumbled as if it had been hit by a tidal wave. Bolting toward the diminishing figure, she cried, "Clay! Clay! Wait!"

Clay was about to ride into the dense forest, his heart feeling like a chunk of ice, when he heard Barbara's call. Pulling rein, he looked back over his shoulder and saw the beautiful woman running toward him, holding her skirt off the ground. He wheeled the pinto around and trotted to meet her, and when they drew abreast, Barbara's tear-stained face shone in the sunlight.

Lips quivering, she looked up at him and said, "I need you to get off the horse."

Clay's heart was thundering in his chest as he slid to the ground. Stepping close to him, Barbara reached up and cupped his face in her trembling hands. Then she sobbed out the words, "I love you, my darling Clay! I . . . I've known it for months, but I was afraid to let you know, afraid that you'd one day hurt me as Jack did. Now I realize how foolish I've been, because I know your love is true and you'd never hurt me!"

For the moment the lump in Clay's throat kept him from speaking, but he could express his joy in another way. Folding the woman he loved into his powerful arms, he pressed her to him and kissed her long and tenderly.

When at last he held her at arm's length, elated, he found his voice, telling her, "You have just made me the happiest man in the world! You wait here with your sister. As soon as I see how it goes with Moxley, I'll be back. If I'm able to find him and make him tell the truth, I'll be a free man. Will you marry me if I can clear myself?"

Looking lovingly into his dark brown eyes, Barbara replied, "Darling, I'll marry you *now* if you want. Even if you have to go back to prison, I'll wait for you and marry you whenever you get out."

Clay kissed Barbara again, then said, "I love you even more for being willing to wait for me. Let's just pray I can find Moxley and make him tell the truth. I don't know how I'm going to force him to do it, because he'll still want to protect his brother—but now you've given me even more incentive to do so."

Kissing her one more time, Clay swung onto the pinto and said, "I'll be back as soon as I can."

Barbara reached out and gripped his arm, pleading, "Let me go with you!"

"No, honey," he said firmly, "it's too dangerous."

"We've been in plenty of danger together before," she parried. "I love you, Clay, and my place is with you, and I want to be with you when you find Moxley. I promise I won't get in the way. I'll stay out of sight when you go to Moxley's cabin, but I want to be near you. Please, darling, let me go with you!"

Clay lifted his hat and ran his fingers through his curly hair. Finally he smiled and looked down at her. "When you put it like that, how can I say no? Let's go tell Susan."

Minutes later the couple was heading westward out of Aspen. Clay glanced back to see if there was any sign of the lone rider, but the man was not in sight. He then looked over at Barbara as she looked at him, her eyes shining with love. Feeling as though nothing could stop him now from achieving his goal, Clay put his horse into a gallop, heading straight for Buckskin Pass.

Chapter Fourteen

Susan Granville watched her sister ride away with the man she loved beside her, and then she went back inside her cabin. Sitting down at a small corner table, she picked up the dress she was making and started stitching. "Barbie, dear," she murmured half aloud, "I sure hope your Clay Edwards can clear himself. He seems a fine man, and I never saw love for you in Jack's eyes like I saw in Clay's."

About half an hour later there was a knock at the door. Putting down her sewing, Susan crossed the room and opened the door. She stared at a tall, slender man in his mid-forties with a U.S. marshal's badge on his vest. Touching his hat brim, he said, "You're Susan Granville?"

"Yes, I am, Marshal," she replied, her heart sinking, knowing what he was there for.

"I'm United States Marshal Lance Cooper, ma'am," the lawman explained. "I've been trailing a man named Clay Edwards. I followed him here to Aspen and did a little asking on the street. Folks told me two riders came in a while ago on Indian pinto ponies. One of them fit Edwards's description. Folks said the other rider was a woman. Said she looked a lot like you. They figured she had to be your sister. That so?"

Susan knew there was no way to cover for Clay, and she could not think of a way to stall the lawman. Reluctantly she nodded, admitting, "Yes, sir."

"I assume they've headed for Buckskin Pass."

"Why, uh . . . yes. Mr. Edwards is trying to find a man named C.K. Moxley so he can prove that he wasn't in on the robbery for which he was convicted and sent to prison. My sister explained that Mr. Edwards was set up to take the blame so that Moxley's younger brother—who was *really* in on the robbery—could go free."

Cooper chuckled dryly, shoved his hat to the back of his head, and said, "Ma'am, with all due respect to your sister, somebody's lyin' through their teeth. I'd rather believe that your sister has been fooled by Edwards into accepting his cock-and-bull story. I'm sure she thinks what you just told me is the truth—but I can assure you it's a pack of lies. The fact is Edwards and Moxley are partners in crime. Edwards holed up somewhere in the mountains for the winter, but now he's on his way to join up with his pal."

Susan stiffened. Fully convinced that Clay Edwards was innocent, she asked, "How can you be so sure that he lied to Barbara? Do you have proof that Mr. Edwards and Moxley are partners?"

"That was proven in court, ma'am, or Edwards wouldn't have been sent to prison."

"Judges and juries have sent innocent men to prison before, Marshal Cooper," countered Susan.

"I realize that, ma'am," Cooper admitted begrudgingly, "but that's not the case here. We've also got testimony from Edwards's cellmate at Canon City. He told the warden after Edwards escaped that Edwards had admitted to him in private he was part of the Moxley gang. Said he was in on the holdup all the way. Matter of fact, he was the one who told us about Moxley's hideout in Buckskin Pass and that Edwards was planning on heading for it."

Susan realized that by pressing the lawman in this manner, she was unwittingly detaining him. If she could keep it up, perhaps Clay could elude the marshal long enough to get Moxley in his hands by the time Cooper got there. "Let me ask you this, Marshal," the young woman went on, "have you—"

"I don't have time to stand here and jaw with you, ma'am," Cooper cut in. "I really must be going. Would you mind telling me exactly how to find Buckskin Pass?"

"Would you just answer one question for me, Marshal?" Susan urged.

Cooper sighed, shifted his feet impatiently, and sourly asked, "What?"

"How much do you know about Clay Edwards? I mean, do you know anything about his life before he was convicted and sent to prison? My sister didn't have time to tell me anything about it, but I'm wondering if he had a criminal record before this robbery."

"Well, ma'am," Cooper replied, clearing his throat, "I know he was a gunfighter, but I seem to remember that this was Edwards's first offense. In fact, I'm sure of it."

"Did you know that Moxley has a brother?"

"No, I didn't know, but—"

"Isn't it possible that Moxley is trying to cover for an outlaw brother, and that Mr. Edwards has taken the blame for him?"

"Anything's possible, ma'am, but it's not my job to speculate. My job is to capture Edwards and Moxley and take them in."

"But shouldn't you give Mr. Edwards a chance to get his hands on Moxley so he can be in a position to make the man tell the truth?" Cooper opened his mouth to reply, but Susan went on forcefully, "What evidence do you actually have? From what Barbara told me, you have the word of a convicted killer that Mr. Edwards was in on the robbery. And you have the word of this cellmate at the prison who obviously has it in for Mr. Edwards for engineering his recapture—a man who is, I might add, *another* convicted killer. Yet you're willing to take their word over that of a man who has no criminal record in the past?" She shook her head in disbelief. "Well, it seems to me—"

"Ma'am, I've got to be on my way. I will ask you again to tell me how to get to Buckskin Pass. If you know and don't tell me, you are guilty of obstructing justice."

Fearful of the consequences, Susan gave him the information, begging, "Please be careful not to harm my sister."

"I'll try, ma'am. I'll try."

A brisk mountain wind cut across the high country as Clay Edwards and Barbara LaBonde rode amid towering, snowcapped peaks. Enjoying the warmth of the sun and taking in the beauty of the Rockies, Barbara remarked. "Susan said Buckskin Pass was almost twelve thousand feet up. Isn't that above the timberline?"

"Sure is," Clay confirmed. "The timberline's somewhere around eleven thousand feet. Higher than that, the oxygen's too thin for plant life to grow."

Scrutinizing the terrain around them, Barbara said, "We must be at least ten thousand feet up right now, wouldn't you say?"

"Yep."

"Then if Moxley's cabin is on this side of the pass, we must be getting close."

"Right again," he responded. Suddenly two young riders came down the trail toward them. Clay froze for a moment, then relaxed. "For a minute there I thought Moxley was coming to greet us, but neither of those fellas is built anything like him. Let's see if they can tell us anything."

As they drew closer, it was apparent that the riders were quite young and clearly related. A small deer was draped over the back of one of the horses, and as Clay came abreast of the young hunters, he drew rein and said, "Howdy. Looks like there'll be meat on somebody's table tonight."

"You're right about that," one of the youths said, grinning, while the other one admired Barbara.

Addressing the one who had spoken, Clay asked, "You fellas from around here?"

"Yep. We live about a mile down this trail off to the south a ways."

Eager for the answer to his next question, Clay said, "We're looking for a man named Moxley. You know him?"

"Didn't exactly know him, mister," replied the young hunter, "but I know where he lived."

Clay's ears sharpened. "Lived?"

"Yes, sir. I'm afraid your trip was a waste of time. We passed near his place a few minutes ago, and there's a fresh grave close to the trail. The date on the marker says he died two weeks ago."

Clay's heart froze. With C. K. Moxley dead, there was no way he could clear himself. His mouth suddenly dry, Clay said to the hunter, "I'd like to see the grave. Is the Moxley place on this side of the pass?"

"Yes, sir," the youth confirmed, twisting in the saddle and pointing due west. "Cabin's no more'n a quarter mile up there, to the right of the trail. It's below the timberline, so you can't see the cabin for the trees, but the grave's in a clearing close to the trail, about fifty or sixty yards this side of the cabin."

Clay thanked the young man and watched the hunters ride on. When they were out of earshot, Barbara nudged her horse close to the stunned Clay and took hold of his hand, saying, "Darling, I know this is a terrible blow to you, but I want to say again that I will wait for you no matter how long you have to be in prison."

Clay managed a smile. He leaned toward her and planted a soft kiss on her lips. "You're one in a million, little lady," he breathed with conviction. Looking then toward Buckskin Pass, he said somberly, "Let's go see the grave."

The disheartened couple rode up the steep trail for a short distance, and then the clearing where the grave was located came into view. Veering off the trail, they rode toward the newly turned mound, which was marked by a crude wooden cross and situated at the edge of the clearing several yards from a huge pine tree. Before reaching the grave, Clay and Barbara caught a brief glimpse of the cabin high up in the trees.

Clay's heart was like lead as he dismounted and then gave Barbara his hand to help her down. Walking toward the grave, bitterness welled up within him, for he knew his only hope of being cleared lay cold beneath the sod.

Suddenly Barbara squeezed his hand and pointed toward the cabin, which could now be seen more clearly. "Look, Clay!" she exclaimed. "There's smoke coming from the chimney!"

Reading the marker, Clay squeezed her hand back and declared excitedly, "It's not C.K. in the grave, Barbara! It's Michael Moxley. By the dates, he was quite a bit younger than C.K.—no doubt the brother I was framed for." Swinging his gaze toward the cabin, he stated through clenched teeth, "C.K.'s in the cabin, honey. You wait here. I'm going after him."

Suddenly a cold voice from the shadows cut through the mountain air. "You're not going anywhere, Edwards! Get those hands up!"

Barbara gasped and Clay spun around to see a tall, slender man emerge from the mottled shade of the pine tree. There was a badge on his vest and a cocked Colt .44 in his hand. Stepping close and removing Clay's gun from its holster, the lawman jammed it under his belt and said, "My name's Lance Cooper, U.S. marshal. You're under arrest."

Holding his hands shoulder high, Clay said, "So you're the one who's been following us."

Cooper lifted his chin in triumph and said coldly, "I've been smelling your scent for a long time, jailbird. Nice of you to lead me to your partner. Now you can *both* go with me—you back to prison, and Moxley to the gallows."

Barbara pressed close to Clay as he said, "Marshal, I know you've heard this from most of the men you've arrested in however many years you've been a lawman, but I am truly innocent, and C.K. Moxley can clear me."

"I don't have time for this!" Cooper rasped, pulling a pair of handcuffs from his hip pocket. "I'm going to chain you to a tree while I go up there and arrest your cohort."

"Marshal, I'm pleading with you," Clay said, looking the man square in the eye. "If you do this, I'll never be able to prove my innocence. Moxley will hold to his story and let you take me back to prison. This man in the grave was probably the brother he was protecting, but Moxley's not going to admit it unless he's forced to."

Cooper jutted his jaw stubbornly. "You're right, Edwards. I've heard this old song and dance ever since I pinned on a badge. What do you think we have courts for? You were tried and convicted in a court of law, duly authorized by the state of Colorado. That's all that matters to me. It's my job to bring you in. If you got a raw deal, tell it to somebody else. I haven't got time for this."

Barbara stepped away from Clay and faced the lawman. Her eyes were filled with tears as she asked, "Marshal Cooper, have you ever known of a jury to be wrong about a man, even when all the evidence pointed to his guilt?"

Cooper sighed. "You sound just like your sister, ma'am. Why don't you just hop on your pony and go on back to Aspen."

Barbara smiled weakly. "So Susan tried to talk sense into your head, too?"

"Yeah, but she didn't succeed any more than you're going to."

"Still, you haven't answered my question."

Nodding, the federal man admitted, "Okay, okay. Yes ma'am, I have known juries to be wrong."

"What if the jury that convicted Clay was wrong? What if he is indeed innocent but you won't even give him a chance to prove it? What will happen when some day the truth finally comes out—for I know that it will—and you realize that you had a part in cutting a big hole out of Clay's life because you were too pigheaded to have a little common sense and maybe a little bit of compassion? Tell me, Marshal Cooper, will your conscience bother you? Will your sleep be disturbed? Or are you so tough you don't need any sleep?"

Clay wanted to applaud Barbara's eloquence, but he remained silent.

U.S. Marshal Lance Cooper was clearly nonplussed. He looked sharply at Barbara, then drawled, "Pigheaded, eh?"

"Pigheaded," Barbara confirmed flatly.

A smile cracked the lawman's thin face. "Ma'am," he said quietly, "if they ever allow females to be lawyers, you ought to consider being one." Looking at Clay, he asked, "How did you plan to force Moxley to tell the truth?"

Clay felt relief wash over him, and it showed in his face. Lowering his hands, he replied, "We'll sneak up there together, but let me go in alone. Listen to our conversation, and when you hear what he says, draw your own conclusions—and your gun, if necessary."

Cooper nodded. "I may lose my badge over this, but your lawyer here has suddenly convinced me that you're innocent." Handing Clay his gun, he added, "Can't let you face the guy unarmed. Let's go."

Barbara smiled at the lawman and breathed, "Thank you, Marshal. You won't regret your decision, I promise you."

Cooper grinned, shook his head, and responded, "You're some kind of woman, ma'am. If I weren't already married, I'd try to court you."

"She's already taken, Marshal," spoke up Clay, "and we're getting married as soon as this thing is settled."

Barbara embraced Clay and warned, "Be careful. Moxley may have a whole gang up there."

Clay kissed her forehead. "I'll be careful, honey. You wait here."

Clay and Marshal Cooper moved stealthily through the dense woods, leaving Barbara LaBonde with the horses. They checked the small barn at the rear and found two horses, but they presumed one of the animals had belonged to Michael Moxley. Making their way to the front of the cabin, they drew up behind a large tree.

"Okay, you get inside, and then I'll sneak up so I can

listen," Cooper instructed. "If you have to shoot him, don't kill him, 'cause if he's dead, I can't hear what you're wanting me to hear."

"Don't worry about that," Clay promised.

The ex-gunfighter drew his gun, thumbed back the hammer, and made a dash for the front porch. Using his momentum, he hit the door hard with his shoulder. It gave way instantly, and he plunged inside.

C. K. Moxley's short, stubby frame was stretched out on a bed in the one-room cabin. He was clad in pants and socks, while his upper body was covered only by his long johns. Caught completely off guard, he sat up with his eyes bulging. His shock was even greater when he recognized the face behind the ominous black muzzle pointed at him. "Edwards!" he gasped.

"On your feet, Moxley!" commanded Clay. "You and I are gonna have us a little talk!"

Clay saw Moxley's gaze flicker to a bureau across the room, the top drawer of which was partly open. Then the stout killer planted his stockinged feet on the floor and stood, wiping a hand over his stubbled face. "Talk?" he asked. "About what?"

"About how you framed me. Your dirty lies have cost me nearly a year out of my life."

Glaring insolently at the ex-gunfighter, Moxley demanded, "So what?"

"So you're going to come clean and tell the truth to the law."

Sneering, the killer mocked, "What're you gonna do if I refuse? Kill me? You ain't no murderer, Edwards. You ain't got the guts. So I ain't tellin' no law nothin'."

Clay did not know if such a veiled admission was enough for Cooper, so he decided he would give him more. Holding the gun steady on Moxley, he said, "I saw the grave out there. Is Michael your brother?"

"Yeah," the squat man said with a nod, his face sobering.

"Is he the one I went to prison for?"

"Yep. Uncanny how much you two were built alike, not to mention you had the same Stetson as Mike." He snorted with derision, remarking, "That dumb sheriff and everybody else sure thought it was you helpin' us rob that bank." Moxley's face suddenly collapsed, and Clay thought he saw the trace of a tear in one eye as he said, "Didn't do my little brother much good, though. He came down with pneumonia about three weeks ago. He only lasted a week."

"But you'd have let me rot in prison just the same, wouldn't you?" Clay asked bitterly.

A look of kindness came over Moxley's face, and he smiled, saying, "Look, I'm startin' to feel bad about what I done to you. It really was a lowdown thing to do. I've got an idea." Moving slowly toward the bureau, Moxley proceeded, "Let's you and me make a deal. I know all about how good you are with a gun. How about us joinin' forces? You're a marked man now. You've got a prison record. You can't go back to society and live a normal life, so let's *really* rob banks together. We'll split everything down the middle."

Clay was following closely with his Colt .45 as Moxley walked closer to the bureau. The killer stopped a step or two away from the bureau and said, "Look, I really do want to make it up to you for what I did. I got a bundle of money right there in that drawer. Put that gun away, and let's be partners, okay? Just to show you my heart's in the right place, I'll give you ten thousand as goodwill money to start off our new partnership."

"I'm not interested," Clay retorted coldly.

Anger immediately showed in the outlaw's eyes. "Don't be a fool, Edwards! I'm offerin' you a good deal! Like I said, you can't live a normal life no more. You're a marked man."

"Not anymore I'm not," Clay said evenly.

Moxley's eyes blazed. "Oh, yes, you are!" he spat. "I'm the only man who can clear you with the law, and I ain't never gonna do it!"

"You already have," the ex-gunfighter said, grinning.

Over his shoulder, Clay called, "I think you've heard enough, Marshal! Come on in!"

As the lawman stepped into the cabin, C. K. Moxley swore and thrust his hand into the drawer. "Don't do it, Moxley!" Clay bellowed, his gun pointed dead center at the outlaw.

Panicked, Moxley pulled a revolver out of the drawer and swung it up at Clay. But Clay instantly fired, and the bullet tore through Moxley's heart. The outlaw fell to the floor, landing on his back, his lifeless eyes staring blankly.

As Clay was holstering his gun, a strong hand clamped his shoulder. "You're a free man, Edwards," said U.S. Marshal Lance Cooper. "I'll—"

"Thank you, Marshal! This is wonderful!"

The two men turned to see Barbara LaBonde standing in the doorway. "I had to be closer," she confessed sheepishly. "I was out there by the porch behind a tree."

Gesturing at Moxley, the marshal suggested, "Let's go outside. No need to have to look at this mangy dog any longer than necessary."

Clay hurried across the room and put an arm around Barbara. "You've got grit, little lady. That's one of the things I love about you." As they stepped outside, Clay saw that Barbara had brought all three horses up close to the cabin.

Turning to Clay, Cooper repeated, "As I was saying, Edwards, you're a free man. I'll ride straight to Denver and wire Warden Ruzek from the U.S. marshal's office. You'll be getting a letter of apology from the state, which will also officially clear you of all charges. Where shall I have it sent?"

Clay looked down at Barbara. Holding her gaze, he told the lawman, "Have them send it to me at the Diamond J Ranch at Gunnison."

While Marshal Cooper stayed behind, checking over Moxley's cabin for stolen money and getting the body ready to haul it back down the mountain, Clay and Barbara led their horses through the trees back to the trail. As they stepped from the trees, the valley was displayed before them, glistening in the sun.

Barbara took a deep breath and exclaimed, "Oh, Clay. It's so beautiful!"

Wrapping her in his arms, he looked into her eyes and said, "Not as beautiful as you." He paused, then mused, "You know, I really should have thanked Moxley for framing me. If he hadn't, I never would have met you."

Laughing, the beautiful brunette concurred. Then she tilted her face up to the tall, rugged man and they kissed tenderly. Hugging him tight, Barbara whispered, "Oh, Clay, I love you so much! With all my heart I love you!"

Grinning crookedly, Clay remarked, "Seems I remember you told me you'd never give your heart to another man."

"I didn't," she countered, devilment in her eyes. "You stole it!"

STAGECOACH STATION 51:
WILD WEST
by Hank Mitchum

In 1899 the Old West is mostly a memory, kept alive by old-timers and touring Wild West shows, two of which are Cactus Corrigan's Great Wild West and the Yakima Kid's Ace-High Pioneer Exposition and Wild West. The troupes' owners, Earl Corrigan and John Travers, were once fellow scouts and good friends, but over the years the competition between their companies has turned them into bitter rivals.

That rivalry peaks when both shows are erroneously booked into Kansas City for the same days. However, two other rivals—publishers Jasper Morton Prescott and William Randolph Hearst—take advantage of the situation. Each man will back one of the troupes in a tournament, and the winner of the contest will determine the winner of the wager: If Hearst's troupe wins, he will get Prescott's Kansas City newspaper; if Prescott's wins, he will get $100,000—which will get him out of debt and keep his newspaper afloat.

But when sabotage tragically prevents the contest from coming to an end, Hearst proposes a solution: an overland stagecoach race, pitting the troupes' drivers from Kansas City to Denver and culminating in a huge Fourth of July celebration. The coaches get under way, but soon they become the target of the saboteur—and the race, originally a test of skill, turns into a battle for survival.

Read WILD WEST, on sale January 1991 wherever Bantam paperbacks are sold.